Angel of Death

Angel of Death

ANTHEA COHEN

PUBLISHED FOR THE CRIME CLUB BY

DOUBLEDAY & COMPANY, INC.

GARDEN CITY, NEW YORK

1985

Library of Congress Cataloging in Publication Data
Cohen, Anthea.
Angel of death.
I. Title.
PR6053.034A74   1985   823'.914
ISBN 0-385-19125-1
Library of Congress Catalog Card Number 84-13599
Copyright © 1983 by Anthea Cohen
All Rights Reserved
Printed in the United States of America
First Edition in the United States of America

Angel of Death

CHAPTER 1

Agnes Carmichael put a saucer of cut turkey breast down on the floor, near the table, for Tibbles. The table was laid for her own lunch: cold turkey, stuffing, a couple of cold chipolatas—the usual lunch thousands of other people would be having, although probably with their families. Carmichael was having it alone—except, of course, for Tibbles.

She had saved herself a glass of wine from the half bottle she had opened yesterday. She sat down and prepared to enjoy her lunch. Christmas Day had been spent alone, but happily. She had tried to make it a real Christmas, with a proper Christmas dinner. The television had been good, the weather bad, but that had not mattered, her little flat was warm and comfortable. Yes, she thought, as she started on her cold turkey, she'd enjoyed it. Only, when the bells had rung on Christmas Eve and she had sat and listened by the electric fire—that had not been quite so good.

This afternoon she was going to have tea with Amy Jones—Sister Jones—her only friend in the hospital, the only one she'd made during her three years there. Carmichael did not particularly like friends; she didn't like anyone to get too close and Amy Jones didn't. She was rather afraid of Carmichael, and Carmichael never hesitated to use her superior rank when necessary. So, she was going to have tea with Jones, today, Boxing Day. Jones couldn't come out; her mother was now completely bedridden. She had to have someone to look after her while Jones was at work. In a way, Carmichael thought she was doing Jones a favour going there to tea. It would brighten up her Christmas a bit.

The cat walked unhurriedly from the kitchen, tail erect. When she saw the plate of turkey breast she began to purr loudly. The cat was quite changed from the emaciated, timid, scrawny creature Carmichael had brought in that night from the pouring rain, from that house. . . . Well, she didn't want to think of that, not at Christmas time, but Tibbles had certainly changed, filled out; she was almost a fat cat now.

Carmichael had filled out a little, too; she was not quite so thin as she had been three years ago. Now she was Nursing Officer. They had soon seen at the hospital that she was efficient, she knew how to keep people in order, she didn't worry whether she was liked or not. As Nursing Officer she wore not an apron, but a navy blue dress and no cap. In a way, Carmichael regretted the cap—it had done something to hide her sparse, fine, sandy hair.

As well as her uniform, her duties were now totally different. She was in charge of Out Patients, the Eye department, Casualty, the Children's Ward, and operating theatres; also responsible for the redistribution of staff. If someone went off sick in one of the departments, she had to replace them with another. It was not a job that always led to popularity, but popularity was not one of the things that mattered to Carmichael. She found the job pleasing and her promotion gratifying. In Carmichael's opinion, nursing had not always been just to her, but now things seemed to have taken a turn for the better.

Tea with Sister Jones this afternoon would be nice. Poor Jones, thought Carmichael complacently. Her nights must be hell; she often came on duty looking white and hollow-eyed after being up with that awful mother again and again. Carmichael was sorry for her, but, after all, she had long ago suggested a remedy. Jones had been quite shocked; she couldn't accept the idea of putting her mother in a home; she was a dutiful daughter —too damned dutiful in Carmichael's opinion, just making a fool of herself. The old lady hardly knew whether it was her daughter looking after her or someone else, she was so gaga— besides, there were other ways of ridding oneself of such a burden. Carmichael wouldn't have hesitated, but when she had hinted at the idea, Jones had nearly fainted, gone quite pale— Agnes Carmichael sipped her wine and smiled as she remembered the look on Jones' face. She went on thinking about it as she finished her lunch and washed up. Thinking of other people's worries and problems always made Carmichael feel happier, more secure.

She arrived at Jones' little terraced house at three-thirty. Amy greeted her enthusiastically. Carmichael knew that the rest of Jones' family kept well away while her mother was in the state she was. Well, they would, wouldn't they, thought Carmichael with contempt.

"Come in, nice to see you. Cold, isn't it?" Jones fussed round, taking Carmichael's coat and scarf and putting them on the hall chair. They walked into the sitting room. Amy had a coal fire, which was crackling cheerfully. Carmichael thought for an instant, I wish I had a coal fire, but then this thought was quickly followed by another—electricity was cleaner; it could be turned on without fuss and no ashes in the morning. No, she was better as she was, but she walked up to the fire appreciatively and held out her hands to it.

"Nice fire, Amy," she said. Jones nodded.

"It's company when I'm down here alone. I must go and put the kettle on."

"How's your mother?" Carmichael had hardly got the words out when there were three bangs on the ceiling—Mother was knocking. Carmichael knew she kept a walking stick beside her bed to summon Jones when she wanted her. Amy Jones gave a resigned shrug.

"Just the same, as demanding as ever. I'll go up and see what she wants before we start. Do sit down." Carmichael made herself comfortable by the fire. After about ten minutes Amy came back into the room.

"When I got up there she didn't remember what she wanted, so she decided it was the commode. I only had her on it about fifteen minutes ago. Oh Lord . . . Anyway, it's all right for the moment." Amy Jones looked determinedly cheerful and disappeared into the kitchen; Carmichael heard the click of the electric kettle as she put it on, then she came back into the room, still talking.

"Do you know I feel I'd rather be on duty? I mean the kids' ward is cheerful; there was nobody in that was very ill . . .

though," she amended quickly, "it was very good of you to let me have it off. It was nice of you to think of Mother. It would have been difficult to ask anyone to stay with her at Christmas; everyone wants to be with their families, of course. How did you enjoy yesterday?"

"Tibbles and I had quite a nice time, and she appreciated the turkey." Carmichael looked reminiscently at the dancing flames. "What wonderful company a cat is; no trouble, but quite a companion." Carmichael looked up—Jones was not listening.

"It's the nights, you see, five times last night she had me up. I'm frightened if I don't go to her she'll try and get out of bed herself and fall down. It's happened before."

Agnes Carmichael did not return to the subject of Tibbles or yesterday again. She sat eating the rather soggy Christmas cake Jones had produced and drinking the weak tea. Pity, she thought, that Amy can't make a decent cup of tea and serve it in pretty china. She looked at the thick, semitransparent cups and shook her head.

Three more bangs sent Jones running upstairs again during the short time they were having tea. As Jones said, it must be like living in hell . . . Thank God, thought Carmichael, I never knew my mother. If I had, if I'd lived with her, she might have turned out like this. Carmichael had seen Mrs. Jones once or twice and didn't particularly want to repeat the experience, but before tea was over she had to.

Jones had returned and they were just finishing their second cup of tea when there were more bangs on the ceiling—Amy leaned back in her chair determinedly.

"She's just showing off, Agnes, because she knows I've got someone here. She's had a cup of tea and I'm not going up again; I've got to try and discipline her. These old people . . . I do try." The tears came to her eyes and her nose reddened. Carmichael was afraid she was going to break down. So boring, she thought; she didn't want that. She rose to her feet.

"Do you want me to go? I will if you like."

"No, no, thanks, let's leave her for a bit. It won't hurt her and she's got to learn." Amy Jones had hardly finished her sentence when there was an almighty crash.

"Oh, gosh, she's fallen out of bed. She's never done that in the day before. It's—it's just because—"

"I'll come up with you. You won't be able to get her back into bed yourself; perhaps she's broken her hip." Carmichael said it lightly with a half smile and Jones looked at her, horrified. "Well," continued Carmichael, "it would mean you'd be rid of her for a bit while they pinned it." She followed a silent, shocked Jones up the stairs.

"Well, thanks for coming anyway. Nice to ask you round to tea on Boxing Day and then your having to cope with this."

Carmichael was amazed at the deterioration in Mrs. Jones since she had last seen her. She'd lost a lot of weight and her hair, which had been quite nicely done, was now straggly and pushed back with two slides. She was lying on the floor beside the bed; between them they picked the old woman up and put her back into bed, Jones holding her mother forward while Carmichael expertly piled the pillows behind her.

"She seems all right. Must keep them sitting up or they get pneumonia and die." Carmichael was aware of a searching look from Amy Jones, looking perhaps for a hint of sarcasm.

"Yes, that's true," Jones said, automatically, lifting her mother further up the bed. "She slides down—you know how they do."

Agnes Carmichael stood back and looked at the old woman. Mrs. Jones' mouth was half open and the inside looked like a black cavern. A few yellow teeth showed. She looked directly in Agnes' direction without recognition. She said, suddenly, in a cracked, husky voice,

"I fell out. You didn't come. I was trying to get to the commode . . . Who's this?"

"I'm sorry, Mother, but you've been out on the commode three times this afternoon and done nothing. This is Miss Carmichael—you remember her. You saw her some time ago; she's from the hospital." The old woman shook her head irritably on the pillow and went on shaking it, beating her hands on the coverlet.

"Nobody cares since your father died. He is dead, isn't he?" She suddenly opened her eyes very wide—they were a pale, washed out blue—and looked at her daughter, confused. Amy

Jones nodded and put her hand over the clawlike one still beating the covers.

"Yes, you know he is, Mum, years ago." Jones looked at Carmichael and raised her eyes to heaven. "Now you won't be a
naughty girl and do that again, will you?" The old woman shook
her head; she seemed to have forgotten about the commode and
why she had been trying to get out of bed—she was, as Carmichael noted, confused.

"She wants cot sides; she ought to be in hospital," said Carmichael brutally in front of the old woman, who heard her and
opened her eyes wide again.

"Hospital! I'm not going to no hospital," she said, her voice
rising. "Got Amy, got a daughter who's a nurse, what more
. . ." Then she seemed to forget the whole matter, closed her
eyes, and slid a little further down the bed.

The two women walked out of the room and downstairs,
Jones registering a little of the disapproval she felt at
Carmichael's remark.

Agnes was glad to get back to her own flat. In spite of the coal
fire, Jones' house had not been warm and Carmichael's feet had
got cold while she had been there. What a setup, she thought,
glad it's not mine.

Tibbles greeted her affectionately. It was raining now, a
nasty, sleety rain. She closed the front door firmly. Tibbles must
not go out in this. She went through into the kitchen. Yes, the
cat had used her box. With the precision of long habit, Carmichael took a jar out of the cupboard under the sink. In the jar
was disinfectant with a spoon standing in it. She spooned out
the soiled granules from the cat's tray into a plastic bag, twisted
the top of the bag and knotted it, then dropped it in the pedal
bin. Cats were so easy . . . poor Jones.

CHAPTER 2

Back at the hospital the next morning Carmichael did her round early. She had left instructions for the staff that she wanted all decorations down and every sign of them away by that morning. Christmas Day and Boxing Day were, in her department, the only time when the place was to be decorated, and the staff, under her supervision, knew she'd brook no nonsense. She went round the Out Patient department looking critically at the ceiling to see if any part of the streamers that had been up remained, stuck there by Sellotape, as they did sometimes. Sister followed her.

"Good; no signs of festivities. That's what I like to see, Sister. Back to work now. Let's hope the men feel the same, particularly Mr. O'Connor, that new Registrar. If he is as late to his Clinics as he was last week, tell me, Sister."

The Sister nodded. "He has some distance to come, Miss Carmichael, he . . ." Sister obviously liked Mr. O'Connor.

"Then he should start out earlier, shouldn't he, Sister?" Carmichael turned on her heel, twitching the navy dress down on her hips. She continued her journey to the Children's Ward.

Sister Jones was sitting at her desk, and she looked tired and pale. Carmichael felt a wave of pleasure wash over her. It was nice to compare her own easy situation with Jones' troubled one; it made her feel so much more comfortable.

"Good morning, Sister Jones," she said formally. One would not have guessed from her manner that the two women had met, had a cup of tea, and coped with Mother yesterday.

"I had a terrible night. Six or seven times she got me up, and I was terrified she'd fall out of bed again if I didn't go." Jones looked up, hoping for sympathy, but she got none.

"Well, you know what I think, Sister—you should put her in a home; she's really not fit to be there. You could pull strings, surely, with one of the consultants, I should have thought. What's the woman like who's looking after her? Reliable?"

Jones nodded. "I have suggested it . . . but, well, you saw what she was like when you mentioned hospital yesterday—she wouldn't go; or to a home . . . she wouldn't have it."

"If she was my mother, she'd have to have it. She must understand that you've got a job to do. And now, let me do my round. I really didn't come here to talk about your mother."

"Sorry, I didn't mean . . . Miss Carmichael," Jones relapsed into the formality that she knew Carmichael liked. They walked round the ward, again Agnes Carmichael looking for any signs of yesterday's Christmas tree, even pine needles on the floor, but there were none; she could find no fault. She spoke to one or two children playing with their Christmas toys. There were only eight in the ward—as many children as possible were sent home at Christmas, and the ones that were in were either recent operations or, in one case, a little boy with a fractured elbow. Carmichael passed the glass-partitioned nursery and looked in at a small child in a cot. She turned to Jones.

"All right, that child?" she asked, and Jones nodded.

"Doing well, considering."

The nurse in the cubicle with the baby, masked and gowned, looked up at them and Carmichael nodded briefly to her and left the ward. As she did so she heard Jones heave a sigh behind her. She knew how she felt, but really it did serve her right—it was ridiculous keeping the old woman at home.

Her next destination was the theatre. She walked up the stairs —Carmichael never used the lift if she could help it and she dissuaded the staff from doing so, not that they took much notice of her. At the top floor she arrived at theatres and looked at the door where the lighted OPERATION IN PROGRESS she felt could be true—or not. She pushed open the door slightly and looked inside. The backs of three green-clad figures were scrubbing up at the sink and through the glass above them she could see two porters lifting a patient on to the operating table. She stepped sideways and had a quick look at the list pinned up by the door.

General Surgery List—December 27th

Mrs. James	Cholecystectomy
Mrs. Leman	Laparotomy
Mr. Freeborn	Removal of lipoma

Not exactly over exerting themselves with that list, thought Carmichael. Then she shrugged. She had little time for surgeons. It was always the same after a holiday; things ground to a halt, then took ages to get up their rhythm again. There should have been six on that list at least. Three scrubbing up, she noted it. The operating lists were really nothing to do with her, but Carmichael liked to keep her eyes open to see who was slacking and to see who wasn't.

What next? The Eye department. This department was slightly separated from the rest of Out Patients. You had to go out into the street, along the road, and in through a door. Over the top in large letters were the words EYE CLINIC. In spite of this, people still drifted about looking for it, Carmichael thought of them with contempt. True, they had to come first to Out Patients to register, but then you'd think . . . but no, you'd find them wandering about down by the Plaster room or the Pharmacy. Patients seemed to lose their knowledge of which was right and which was left in hospitals, in spite of the notices.

Carmichael pushed open the Eye Clinic door and looked into the small waiting room. This was a pleasant place, the only part of the department that was carpeted; the chairs, too, were more comfortable than in the large waiting room, perhaps in deference to the patients' disabilities. She looked round at the assembled patients, some with a patch over one eye, some in dark glasses. She looked toward the Clinic door, then turned to go out back into the street, and back into the hospital—when suddenly something stopped her.

Seated in a chair, slightly apart from the other patients, was a man . . . a man in whose arms she had rested for a few seconds . . . how long ago? Three years at least, but she hadn't forgotten . . . she hadn't forgotten his deep voice as he had held her and explained that he was blind, this was why he had bumped into her. Carmichael stood as if she was rooted to the spot, gazing at him.

The woman sitting beside him Carmichael supposed was his wife. She was smartly dressed, handsome, her face full of impatience. She looked directly at Carmichael and obviously recognized someone in authority, someone not wearing an apron.

"May I ask how long we're going to wait here? Our appointment was for nine o'clock. That's bad enough getting here at that time, but it's half past ten now—we've been waiting here well over an hour."

"What name is it?" Carmichael went up close to the pair, still keeping her eyes on the man's face. Was it her imagination or did he, at the sound of her voice, turn towards her as if he remembered. She dismissed the thought with reluctance as ridiculous.

"It's Maitland, Professor Harold Maitland. He's to see the Consultant, not anyone else."

"I'll . . ." Carmichael tore her eyes away from his face. "I'll go and see what's happened, Mrs. Maitland, if you'll just wait a moment. I'll go to the nurse and see what the hold up is." Carmichael turned, crossed the waiting room, and tapped on the door of the consulting room, which was opened abruptly by a Staff Nurse. Carmichael entered.

"Why has Professor Maitland been waiting so long, Staff?" Carmichael asked softly.

The nurse replied also in a whisper. "He's not here yet, Mr. Ealing. He's late. He told me to make the first appointment for nine o'clock and I told the office and they did, and now in a minute all hell will break loose. There's that Mrs. Winters—she thinks she's a private patient—she'll start I can tell you, Miss Carmichael. Who were you asking about?" She ran her finger down the list on the desk. "Oh, Professor Maitland. God knows when he'll be seen; he's an old patient."

"All right, nurse. Well, I'll try and explain." At that moment Mr. Ealing walked in, slamming the Clinic door behind him.

"Sorry I'm late, nurse. I couldn't help it. Bloody car wouldn't start. I had to get on to the garage and in the end had to get a taxi. That's going to be nice—hospital won't pay for it."

He threw his coat over the back of a chair, shrugged on a white coat, and sat down at his desk.

"Come on then, let's start, for God's sake," he said, irritably.

The nurse switched off the ceiling light, leaving him his desk light, and the light over the letters reflected in the mirror on the opposite side of the wall. She called in the first patient and the Clinic started. Carmichael went out to try and explain the delay to all the patients sitting in the waiting room, but to the Maitlands in particular. Mr. Ealing was a full-time Consultant and did not see patients privately. This meant that people like the Maitlands and Mrs. Winters had to wait their turn like the rest.

"I'm so sorry, Mr. Ealing was detained. A case . . . he had to —" Mrs. Maitland did not wait for Carmichael to finish.

"Well, I'm going. I can't stay here; I can't waste my entire morning. I'm playing bridge this afternoon, so I'll come back, in what—a couple of hours?" This was said sarcastically, but Carmichael did not contradict her.

It might well be a couple of hours if anything happened to delay Mr. Ealing further. The smartly dressed woman gathered up her handbag and shopping bag and swept out without another glance or remark to her husband.

Carmichael turned to him and spoke again, still hoping, praying, that he'd say, "Haven't I heard your voice somewhere before?" After all, blind people were very sensitive to voices, but he didn't. She looked again at his face. It was exactly as she remembered it. She had only seen him for seconds, outside the Catholic church. She'd bumped into him and he'd held her, just for seconds, and she'd carried the memory with her. She didn't know until now how well, how perfectly, the face of this man had been left photographed on her brain. She felt her heart beating faster, faster; it was an extraordinary feeling and something quite new to Carmichael. On impulse she sat down and gently touched his sleeve, he turned quickly.

"Is that . . . ?"

"It's Miss Carmichael. I'm a Nursing Officer, I'm very sorry this has happened. I'll be round again. I'll come back and see you're not forgotten. Perhaps you would like me to bring you a cup of coffee later."

"How very kind of you."

His deep voice lapped round Carmichael like warm water. She would come back, although it really wasn't her job. She had plenty to do in her office—she was, after all, an administrator now, no longer a nurse—but she would come back. She must see him again. Greatly daring, she pressed his arm a little more firmly.

"I'll be back in about three quarters of an hour to see how it's going." Again he thanked her warmly. His smile was sincere and he smiled directly at her, guided, she supposed, by her voice.

"Yes, well . . ." Carmichael was suddenly embarrassed. She got up and left the department, looking back at him sitting quietly in the chair, a big, handsome man, whose imprint had remained with her for three long years. She shook herself and started to run rather unnecessarily fast up the stairs to her office. Once there, her flushed face and nervous, preoccupied manner made Miss Johnson, her companion Nursing Officer, look at her curiously.

"Anything the matter?" she asked.

Carmichael shook her head. She felt bemused. She could still see his face, his white hair. She could still hear the beautiful voice. She shook herself mentally and looked at Johnson.

"No, just the Eye department an hour and a quarter late. Mr. Ealing has only just arrived. I must go back and see how they're getting on shortly." She wished she hadn't said that; there was no need to explain.

"Oh, Mr. Ealing—he's not bad as a rule, is he?" Johnson said. "Still, I'm glad you've got the Eye department rather than me. I know nothing about eyes."

"Yes, I'll go back later." Carmichael's voice trembled and again Miss Johnson looked at her curiously. Carmichael could see her thoughts flitting across her face. It was as if she was saying, "Funny woman; can't understand her."

Both women bent over their administrative tasks. Carmichael drew towards her a pile of procedure sheets she'd got to check and silence reigned in the small office.

CHAPTER 3

Carmichael furtively watched the hands of the electric clock on the office wall. After three quarters of an hour had dragged by she rose to her feet.

"I'm just going to slip down to the Eye department and see whether they've caught up a bit." Johnson didn't even look up.

As she approached the door of the Eye department waiting room Carmichael felt her legs go unaccountably weak. Her knees seemed to tremble and her heart began to race. Just to see him again, just to . . . She wondered if Mrs. Maitland had returned. She hoped not. She hoped he would still be sitting there so that she could get him a cup of coffee from the Canteen, talk to him . . . These plans flew through her mind as she pushed open the door—but his seat was empty. She decided he had either gone home or, perhaps, was in with Mr. Ealing.

As the eye specialist had been over an hour late, it was rather surprising if Professor Maitland had already been seen, but perhaps . . . Probably he was working fast to catch up. At that moment the door of the Eye Clinic opened and Maitland came out accompanied by a junior nurse.

"There's your chair, Mr. Maitland, just ahead of you," said the small nurse cheerfully, relinquishing his arm.

Carmichael longed to go over, take his hand, correct the nurse, and say, "Professor Maitland." The feeling she had was so new to her, she couldn't handle it with ease. She felt she must hold herself in check and stood watching him make his way across the room, and when he had almost reached the chair she went forward.

"Are you all right, Professor Maitland?" she asked, trying to keep her voice steady. What was the matter with her, for goodness' sake, what was the matter?

"Oh, is that the—what did you say?—Nursing Officer?" Harold Maitland held out his hand and Carmichael took it. It was warm and firm. She led him the short way to his chair and he sat down, smiling.

"Can I get you a cup of coffee now?" she asked and he nodded.

"That would be nice. I don't expect my wife will be back yet; she's shopping. I was seen a little sooner than I expected," he said.

"I don't expect it will be very good coffee." She tried to make her voice light, and indeed it was lighter than usual because she was smiling—a rare thing with her.

"Oh, it doesn't matter."

"I'll go and get it, I won't be a moment."

He nodded and Carmichael left the department, went round to Out Patients to the Canteen, ignoring two nurses whom she heard say plainly as she passed, "What's old Carmichael doing here? She's done her round."

They didn't matter. Another time she would have come down on them hard and heavy and said something like "What did you mean by that, nurses?" But not this morning.

She collected two cups of coffee. Why not have one with him? It didn't matter; it would be more companionable. The Eye Clinic was beginning to empty, and anyway they would think she was a friend of his. She paid for the coffee and carried the cups carefully back so as not to spill any in the saucers. She sat down beside Harold Maitland, taking his hand again and guiding it toward the saucer—he took it easily, deftly feeling round the cup for the handle.

"Thank you." He smiled again at Carmichael. He was just about to sip the coffee, the smile still on his lips, when Mrs. Maitland walked through the front door of the department.

"You still here, Miss—er—?" she said to Carmichael. "How very kind of you. Haven't you been seen yet, Harry?"

"Yes, I have, darling," he said, looking in the direction of his wife's voice. "Ealing thinks—"

"I've no time to listen to what Mr. Ealing thinks. Now, please drink that coffee and come—it's late, you know. We've got to get back, have lunch and then I've got to get to Zoë's—that takes half an hour at least. If I'm to get a game of bridge this afternoon at all, we've got to go now."

Harry Maitland's face completely changed. The smile vanished. Carmichael watched him. She felt her hand holding the cup and saucer begin to shake with anger and with horror for how he must feel. She watched him, then turned towards Mrs. Maitland.

She was standing, looking down at her husband, her long white fingers tapping the leather side of her handbag impatiently.

"You don't want that coffee—you don't like instant coffee anyway. You won't drink it at home, so why here?" She took it from his hand and placed the cup and saucer on the window ledge, hardly casting a glance towards Carmichael. Harry Maitland rose immediately.

"All right, darling, if you're in a hurry," he said. The "darling" cut through Carmichael like a knife.

"I managed to park the car right outside," Mrs. Maitland said. "I'm not supposed to, but it'll be all right for a moment if we go straight away. Come on, please hurry."

He followed her, she putting her hand back to take hold of his as they went through the Eye Clinic door. He seemed to have forgotten Carmichael, or so she thought. But as she went forward to hold the door open for him, he turned vaguely, in what he thought was her direction but which was actually looking passed her, and said, "Thank you, Nurse—Miss Carmichael, isn't it?"

Then he turned back and she watched them walk toward the large, green Rover. She watched Mrs. Maitland open the door on the passenger's side and saw him get in with the ease of long practise, but his face was serious. Carmichael saw he was no longer smiling as he had smiled at her. Mrs. Maitland slammed the door and went round to the driving seat. Carmichael watched them draw away from the edge of the kerb. She felt a depression she could hardly control. That bitch! That bitch of a woman—not even to listen to him, not even to wait while he drank the coffee she had got for him . . . *Bitch!* If it had been her, Carmichael, she would have waited—she wouldn't have

wanted to have gone and played bridge, she would have . . .
But what was the use; it wasn't her. She must go back to her
office, but before she did so she had to do something—to find out
. . . She crossed the waiting room and tapped on Mr. Ealing's
door, which was now shut. The nurse opened it, cautiously,
then seeing who it was, slid out.

"Yes, Miss Carmichael?" she said.

"Has Professor Maitland got to come back again—to see Mr.
Ealing?"

"In about six months, I think," the nurse said. "Shall I go and
look?"

"Thank you, no, nurse. I'll find out myself. He's—he's a
friend of mine . . . I see you've caught up a bit. That's good—
that's why I came down." Again Carmichael found herself making the unnecessary explanation, and she chided herself.

Why did she do it? Admittedly, it was unusual for her to do
two rounds in a morning of a department, but, still, she was her
own . . . she could do what she liked; it was nothing to do with
anybody else.

Before she went back to her office she went round to the
Records department to find out the date and time of Harry
Maitland's next appointment. "Harry," she said softly to herself
as she made her way to the Records office, "Harry." That was
what his wife had called him: "Harry." Carmichael hardly recognized herself—that for the first time in her lonely life she was
in love—and like all lonely women it had hit her hard. How
hard she hardly yet realized.

In the Records office she found out that the appointment was
indeed as the nurse thought, six months ahead. She felt she
couldn't wait that long before seeing him again, so she also
noted his address. As she walked back to her office she thought
she would drive round to the address in the appointments book.
She would drive round there and look—just look—at the house
where he lived. It would not be much but it would be something.

CHAPTER 4

During the afternoon, when the other Nursing Officer was doing a round and Carmichael had the office to herself, there was a timid knock on the door.

"Come in."

Sister Jones entered, looking anxiously across at Johnson's desk and showing obvious relief that Carmichael was alone.

"Yes, what can I do for you?" Carmichael's voice was still warm from the morning's encounter and Jones looked encouraged.

"Well, I've come to ask you a favour. I had to go home at lunchtime so I couldn't see you then, so I hope you won't mind my coming to your office . . . It's a personal favour; nothing to do with hospital. I hope you won't mind, but I had to ask you today."

"All right, what is it?" The unusual warmth and demeanour of Carmichael surprised Jones.

"You look—sort of happy. Has anything nice happened?" she asked and Carmichael suddenly looked embarrassed. Did it show? She shook her head and tried to resume her normal, rather waspish, expression, but it was difficult.

"Well, yes . . . in a way. But what is it you want?"

"I hardly like to ask you," Jones said and a trace of irritation broke through Carmichael's euphoria.

"Well, if you don't ask me, I'll never know what it is, so come on."

"Well, on Thursday night there's a concert—Bach—at Lyttleton Hall. There's a marvellous orchestra coming to play and I've got a friend—a woman friend—who's got tickets and she's asked me to go with her."

"So—?" Carmichael looked up at her, waiting for her to go on. She had not asked Jones to sit down.

"My friend has offered to pick me up and bring me back so I won't have to use my car. I thought—you wouldn't—you couldn't—sit for me, could you? I'll give Mum sleeping pills before I go. We would leave at about seven. We're going to have a meal first. I could settle Mum down and she wouldn't wake up. Well, I hope not anyway—sometimes she sleeps right through till morning. I'd be home by twelve." The request obviously meant a tremendous amount to Jones. Normally Carmichael would have dismissed it with one word: no. But today it was different, everything was different; she felt a different person—soft, kind, ready to help anyone.

"All right, I'll do it. I'll come to your house about quarter to seven, and you'll be back by twelve. I don't want to be any later than that."

Jones didn't answer for a second or two; it had been so easy, so . . . She had had to screw her courage up all the morning to ask Carmichael, and she never dreamed . . . And this, this immediate acceptance of the idea—well, it wasn't like Carmichael.

"Oh, thanks! You don't know how much I want to go to this concert. I mean, I never dreamed . . . to get the tickets, well, that was wonderful. Then, I haven't seen this friend for ages. She's from Manchester Hospital and it's going to be so nice and such a lovely treat—you just don't know. I hope I'm not asking too much?"

Carmichael shook her head. "That's all right. What day did you say?" She bent down by the side of her chair and picked up her handbag, took out a small diary, and Jones gave her the date and time again. Carmichael saw in her diary that she was doing nothing all the week. That was hardly unusual—she had few enough dates. She filled in the details, looked up at Jones, and actually smiled.

"I'll do it. Don't worry—you can go to your concert." Jones looked as if she was going to sink down beside Carmichael's chair and continue her thanks. Carmichael waved her hand in dismissal. She wanted to go back to her thoughts of him, Harry Maitland, and bask in the warmth of his remembered presence.

"Thanks, thanks again," Jones said fervently. Seeing the dismissal in Carmichael's face she made for the door and turned again as she opened it with another murmured "Thanks."

That evening Carmichael decided that she would drive the Mini along his street. She felt keyed up with anticipation, as if she was going actually to see him, as if she was going again to feel the warmth of his hand. Yet it was enough at the moment to see where he lived. She had noted down the address carefully, in the same diary in which she had filled in the date she was going to cover for Jones. This evening she would see the garden path down which he walked out of the house when he was going to the University to lecture, then back in the late afternoon or evening. She would see the door, she would see . . .

Johnson came back into the office and Carmichael hastily pulled a list of diet sheets toward her to check what the Sisters had been ordering, to see that no one had ordered too many eggs or too much butter. For the moment she slipped back into her own role, almost, but without the usual hope of finding a mistake in someone else. There was a tender feeling in her she was not used to and that was altering the way she thought; for the moment anyway.

"That young S.E.N. Brown—do you know her?" As Carmichael didn't answer but looked at her in a preoccupied way, Johnson went on. "She went into hysterics in the middle of the ward. Charming. I've sent her off duty to go and see her own doctor. Boyfriend trouble or something, I suppose. But really, she's better away from the place than carrying on like that." Carmichael made some vague reply and Johnson looked at her curiously and then sat down at her own desk and started writing.

That evening Carmichael found the road and found the house. It was large, attractive, the dark oak front door topped by a transom, beautifully shaped windows. As she sat in the Mini opposite the house, watching—she didn't know quite for what, just watching—a light sprang up in one of the windows. Carmichael almost ducked down in her car, then thought, why should a Mini parked on the other side of the road mean anything to anyone in the house? For the moment there was a silhouette at the window, then the curtains were drawn. That must be her, she thought; he wouldn't need a light. Her heart squeezed inside her chest in pity for him.

Carmichael sat there for about half an hour, watching. Nothing else happened. The front door did not open, no more lights came on, no one approached the house. Perhaps he had already come home. Carmichael tried to picture him, sitting in an armchair, perhaps, gazing in front of him with those sightless eyes. She drove away, accompanied by a terrible sense of loss and disappointment—and yet, what had she expected? She thought again of his wife. Was he happy? Surely he couldn't be, not with a woman who hurried him along, as she had in the hospital, who thought going to play bridge was more important than what the eye specialist had told him. Carmichael would never do that to him. She would stay with him, read to him—well, she could imagine it, but that was all she could do. The loneliness she had managed to cope with flooded back over her.

When she got to her flat, she went in and shut the door and leaned against it for a second, then hung up her coat and went along to the sitting room. Tibbles was lying full length on the settee. She went over, picked her up, and held her in her arms, tightly. So tightly that the cat rebelled, struggled, jumped from her arms and made towards the kitchen. Mechanically, Carmichael followed the cat, took a tin of cat food from the cupboard, opened it, put some on a saucer, and placed the saucer on the floor. She watched the cat as it started to eat hungrily; then she went into the sitting room and sat down.

She was aware that she was feeling again the old familiar waning of confidence that she had hardly felt at all since she had been promoted to Nursing Officer. She hated the feeling. For a fleeting second she almost wished Harry Maitland didn't exist. He had made promotion, seniority, her job, fade into insignificance. But no, it was only a fleeting second, and again she was glad he existed. She was glad he was in the same world as she was, even if his coming into her life had meant that all her deficiencies—in looks, in mind, in everything—appeared to be accentuated again. To win a man like that away from his wife, she, Carmichael! And yet, perhaps . . .

She went into the bedroom and looked at herself in the mirror. What had she to offer any man? She looked at her sandy hair, the pointed, sharp nose, the thin lips, and the flat, almost nonexistent bust. He might not be able to see, but he could feel —even if he couldn't see, he could feel. But his hands would never be laid on her, never. She turned away from the mirror and felt the tears stinging behind her eyes.

CHAPTER 5

When Carmichael arrived at Amy Jones' house on the Thursday evening, Jones was in a flutter. She had on a hideous purple dress with beads all over the shoulders and bust, but as Carmichael looked at her, she automatically thought, the bust was big and well proportioned, and she wondered fleetingly why Jones had never . . . but then she supposed it was Mother.

"I've given her two sleeping pills and settled her down and she's fast asleep. She had her supper early, poor old dear, but it had to be done. I couldn't have you summoned up there every five minutes. She may sleep till midnight."

Carmichael nodded, and Jones went on, "My friend will be here at seven, so we've got a minute or two. Would you like to come upstairs and look at her?"

They went upstairs. Jones gently opened the bedroom door. Carmichael peered in, Jones watching her anxiously to see any expression on Carmichael's face that might tell her that things weren't just as they should be. The old lady, dimly visible in the light from a small electric night-light, was lying on her side in the bed, well propped up by the pillows. She was snoring gently. On the table beside her was a glass of orange juice. Carmichael noticed the commode and hoped she wouldn't have to drag the old lady out on it, almost regretting she said she'd come. However, it was done now; it would have to be got through.

Jones was plainly excited. Music must mean a lot to her, Carmichael thought idly. I wonder why it doesn't to me? Carmichael read little, listened to no music, and was not terribly interested in television although she watched it.

"You see, I've done everything I can so that you'll be quite peaceful. She truly doesn't usually wake up till about two. Oh, that's her usual time," said Jones with a trace of bitterness in her voice. "Then she gets me up, to get on the commode, or asks for a cup of tea, or something. Sometimes she's quite lucid and at other times she's very confused."

Carmichael again nodded. "All right, don't worry," she said.

Jones pulled the door to, softly, leaving it ajar so that Carmichael could hear downstairs if the old lady made any movement. She had noticed the stick at the ready by the bedside. If she heard the knock with which she was familiar from visiting Jones, she would go up. They went downstairs quietly. Jones went over and switched on the colour television and pulled the chair a little nearer the coal fire.

"Oh, I almost forgot. I've left you some supper, all ready on a tray in the kitchen. Have it when you feel like it."

"Oh, you really need not have gone to all that trouble," said Carmichael.

Now the evening was here she wanted it over; she wanted Jones to go. Jones noticed the impatience and the difference in Carmichael's attitude from that day she had asked her and found a smiling, warm, Carmichael. Now the old one was back—irritable, unsmiling.

"You're sure you don't mind?"

Carmichael shook her head again irritably and Jones went into the hall, gathered up her coat, and at that moment they heard a car give a small hoot outside.

"That'll be Miriam. Would you like to come out and meet her?" Carmichael shook her head again and Jones gave her a long look. "I hope everything is going to be all right."

"Off you go, Jones. Of course everything is going to be all right."

Jones sidled out of the front door, shutting it softly in case her mother should hear, though after two sleeping pills she thought it unlikely, but with Mother, you never knew.

Carmichael stood in the hall long enough to hear the slam of the car door and the revving up of the engine. Then she walked back into the sitting room and sat down. Athletics on television —she would look at that; you didn't have to think about it, you could dream at the same time. Dreams of the kind she was having now were so new to her. She sat there, imagining walking along the road, arms linked, with the man with the white stick. Perhaps he wouldn't carry the white stick if she . . . Her dreams went on.

The fantasy of Harry Maitland was growing, but instead of making her happy, she was beginning to feel resentful of the fact that she had no beauty to offer him, no confidence, no . . . she hesitated to use the word—thinking of Amy Jones and her love of music—no culture. Anyway, it was useless because of that beastly wife.

The supper Jones had left was good—cold chicken and a salad with nuts and pineapple. Carmichael ate it mechanically, but she had to admit that Jones had taken trouble. She was just finishing the supper and had looked at the time—nine o'clock—not too bad. Two hours had gone, three more to go, when she heard two bangs on the ceiling above her.

"Damn the old woman," she said to herself, "I wonder what she wants. I wonder how confused she'll be when she sees it's not Amy?" She put the tray aside, went upstairs, and pushed open the bedroom door.

"Where's Amy? What's happened?" the old woman looked at her suspiciously but lucidly, her eyes darting round the room as if expecting to see her daughter hiding somewhere.

"I'm looking after you for the evening. Amy asked me to. She's gone to the concert—don't you remember?"

"The concert—the concert—oh, yes."

"What do you want, Mrs. Jones? Tell me—I'm a nurse too. What do you want?"

"The commode, I want the commode. I've got the stomach ache."

Was it the old ploy, wondered Carmichael? She threw back the bedclothes from the skinny legs, swung them over the bed, and helped the old lady onto the commode, automatically straightening the bed and fluffing up the pillows as the old lady sat there. Then, there was an explosion and a terrible smell.

"Oh Lord." Carmichael let the words slip out involuntarily. The old lady appeared to have heard her for she gazed at her

with hostility, then started to struggle upright. Carmichael hastily looked round for a toilet roll.

Mrs. Jones, safely back in bed, relaxed on her pillows as if she
was ready for sleep again.

Carmichael took the old fashioned china pail out of the commode, carried it along to the lavatory, emptied it, rinsed it out,
adding a drop of Dettol. She went back to the bedroom, replaced
the pail in the commode, her face wrinkling with disgust, a disgust which she did not attempt to hide. It was a long time since
she'd had anything to do with bedpans and commodes.

She looked at Mrs. Jones and caught the old lady's eyes fixed
on her. She automatically pulled the bedclothes up more com-
fortably over the old woman and Mrs. Jones shut her eyes, a
strange expression on her face.

Downstairs Carmichael didn't feel like finishing up the small
amount of supper left.

Half an hour passed and then the bangs again. They wakened
Carmichael from a kind of torpor into which she had sunk
watching television. She got up, went upstairs, and as she
opened the bedroom door the smell hit her again. This time, she
knew, the old lady had banged her stick on the floor too late.
Carmichael certainly hadn't bargained for this, and she was an-
gry.

Again, she pulled the old lady out of bed, this time none too
gently, sat her on the commode and proceeded to clean up the
bed. She took the soiled sheet into the bathroom, rinsed it
through in the hand basin, put the plug in, and left the sheet
soaking in hot water. Back in the bedroom she found the old
lady had toppled off the commode and onto the floor. It was
obvious she hadn't hurt herself; she had just crumpled forward
and slithered down. She looked up at Carmichael accusingly, as
if to say she shouldn't have left her; perhaps she was right.

Carmichael put her arms determinedly under the old woman,
pulled her upright, and almost threw her across the bed; then
picked her legs up and thrust those down under the bedclothes,
then remembered she hadn't got a clean drawsheet. Where were
they kept? She found a cupboard in the hall outside the bedroom
which contained a whole pile of these small sheets. She took one

back into the bedroom, rolled the old woman over with little ceremony, inserted the sheet, then rolled her back again, and pulled it through. As she tucked the sheet in, she hoped this wasn't going to happen again.

"Don't do that again, Mrs. Jones," she said. Her voice was harsh. The old woman opened her eyes and looked at her.

"I know you. You're the one who told Amy I should go into hospital, didn't you. I heard you—I heard you. What do you know about anything? I suppose your mother was shoved into a home the moment she got ill. Or perhaps she's dead or maybe you never had a mother—you don't look as if you had." Carmichael would not tolerate this.

"Be quiet, Mrs. Jones. I came here out of kindness, so just be quiet and go to sleep. God knows Amy doesn't get out much—she's tied to you all the time. If the nights are like this, it must be Hell." Carmichael hadn't meant to say quite so much, but the emotion of the last few days seemed to well over and it was nice to take it out of someone.

"Don't talk to me like that. I know your sort—you get a bit of power over at that hospital and you think you're somebody. Well, you're not—you're just a scrawny, ugly old maid, that's what you are." Mrs. Jones even managed to sit up a little, her old face vindictive. Then she collapsed, exhausted, back on to her pillows.

Carmichael's manner suddenly changed. "I'll get you a glass of milk, Mrs. Jones, a nice, warm glass of milk," she said.

She went from the room trembling with rage. How dare that ghastly old woman speak to her like that! How dare she! She'd fix her up for the rest of the night. She went downstairs and warmed some milk and took it up, taking the cup and saucer into the bathroom. A couple more sleeping pills—that's what that old woman needed. Carmichael opened the mirror-fronted bathroom cabinet.

Nembutal—that wasn't often given now—probably the only thing that would work with Mrs. Jones. Mogadon was all the thing now. This old woman had probably been on Nembutal forever. Carmichael took the bottle cap off and emptied two capsules into her hand. Then, about to screw the cap back on, she stopped. She looked at the contents and emptied more into her hand and, almost like an automaton, began to pull the capsules apart, emptying their contents into the milk. One, two, three. When she got to eight she looked at the bottle, shook it, and stopped. She screwed on the top and put the bottle back in the cupboard in exactly the same place as she had found it. She stood thinking for a moment, then decided she would put in two more. She took the bottle out again, broke two more capsules into the milk, then put the bottle firmly back and closed the door of the cabinet. She slipped the empty capsules into her cardigan pocket, but she was not satisfied yet. Jones might notice—ten capsules made quite a difference in the bottle. Carmichael looked round the bathroom and saw what she needed. Carefully she tore off two sheets of toilet paper, emptied some talcum powder on to them, and filled six of the capsules. Opening the cabinet door again she took out the bottle, unscrewed it, placed the talcum filled capsules back into the bottle, and gently shook it so that they would mix nicely with the others. As she did it, she smiled, feeling clever, feeling efficient, feeling confident. She noticed that the talcum powder had made a pleasant smell in the bathroom, so she opened the bathroom window. It would be gone, that pleasant smell, overridden by the worse ones, by the time Amy Jones returned.

Stirring the cup of milk vigorously as she took it back into the room, Carmichael spoke again to the old woman, this time quite gently.

"Here we are, a nice cup of milk."

The old woman struggled to get upright. She looked confused, and when she saw the milk, at first she shook her head. Carmichael sat down on the bed beside her and put her arm firmly round the old woman's shoulders.

"Nice milk," she said, "from an ugly old maid for a gaga, senile old woman." Mrs. Jones looked at her vaguely.

"Drink it," said Carmichael.

Mrs. Jones took the cup and, watching Carmichael almost fearfully over the rim of the cup, she swallowed. Carmichael put her hand under the bottom of the cup and tipped it up so that

the very last of its contents went into the old mouth. As the last
of the milk disappeared, Carmichael smiled again.

This time she settled Mrs. Jones down with quite a degree of
tenderness. Two Jones had given her and ten she had given her;
that should be enough.

Carmichael felt the horrible inadequacy that had been flood-
ing over her since meeting Harry Maitland disappearing. She
took the cup and saucer and the spoon downstairs, washed them
up, and put them away. Twice she went upstairs to look at Mrs.
Jones, who was lying on her side, peacefully sleeping—she was
snoring rather loudly, but that, thought Carmichael smugly,
was to be expected.

At twelve o'clock Jones came in, her worried face appearing
round the sitting room door before her ample body.

"Everything all right?" Carmichael rose to her feet looking at
Jones. She could feel that she had a rather peculiar expression
on her face which she tried to smooth away.

"Yes, everything; quite all right. What a nice supper you left
me."

"Oh, I'm so glad you liked it. I thought perhaps she might
wake up and give trouble."

Carmichael did not reply, but then asked, "Enjoy the concert?
And the dinner?"

Jones' face exploded with delight. "Oh, it was marvellous.
You've never heard anything so wonderful . . . The orch—"
she started, but Carmichael cut her off.

"You must tell me all about it some other time. I'm tired
now."

"Yes, yes, of course."

Jones accompanied her to the door, helped her on with her
coat, and was profuse in her thanks. Carmichael was bored with
the reiterated thank-yous. She went out and got into her car,
looked up at the window. The night-light that Jones always left
on for her mother gleamed feebly. She smiled to herself,
straightened her shoulders; she felt so much—so much better.
She put the car into gear and drove away.

Next morning Sister Jones did not turn up for duty. Carmichael received a phone call when she got to her office, saying

that Sister Jones had phoned in saying that her mother had died in the night. Having received the message, Carmichael put down the phone and bent down to pick up her bag. She took out her compact and looked at herself. This morning her nose didn't look quite so pointed. She had decided to back comb her hair a little more and make it look thicker and the experiment had been a success. She patted it. She looked down complacently at her figure. Her bust might not be very big, but her waist was nice and trim.

CHAPTER 6

During the following week Carmichael did the friendly things. She phoned Jones, but did not get her. Some elderly voice, male, answered her: "Yes, Amy was recovering from the shock. The funeral was etc., etc."

Carmichael then wrote a brief note to Jones saying how sorry she was and how much, she knew, she would miss her mother. She wrote this letter with her lips slightly curled in amusement. She went to the funeral.

It was at the crematorium. Carmichael had not been there before: she had no relatives to lose, nor many friends. She walked with curiosity through the glass doors that led to the small, flower-decked foyer, on through more glass doors, into what looked like a small church, again discreetly flower-decked. Ahead of her, beyond the two symmetrical rows of pews, purple velvet curtains hung as if across a stage, a gold cross in the middle, severely nondenominational. At the side, and at this Carmichael shuddered slightly, was a coffin on a raised structure, surrounded again by flowers; more flowers on the top of the coffin, which was a pale, anaemic, cream wood.

Carmichael slipped quietly into one of the pews at the back and looked round her. There were very few people. In the front seat she picked out Jones' back view. She looked different; fat still, but her back slightly rounded, older. She had her head in her hands. Beside Jones was a large, broad-shouldered man, also fat—probably a brother. Carmichael was not sure how many brothers and sisters Jones possessed, but from the row of fat people, she deduced quite a few, none of whom had helped Jones much. Now they had come round—Carmichael grimaced —like bees round a honeypot. She wondered if Jones would get the house.

These thoughts were accompanied by soft, piped music. Suddenly the priest, or vicar, came out from a side door somewhere near the purple curtains and started to talk. Carmichael shut off; she didn't want to listen. When his talk was over and he retired, everybody stood up, but not before the coffin had been trundled rather noisily through what looked to Carmichael a kind of serving hatch, the doors of which shut silently behind it. Everyone piled out to look at the floral tributes. Carmichael, herself, had sent one and she looked for it amongst the wreaths. Yes, in very good taste, she thought; just a sheaf of scarlet and white flowers —the nurses' colours, which signified death; carnations, their stalks tied with a small, scarlet bow; and the card, "Miss Carmichael, with sympathy." Sympathy! Amy Jones ought to be damn glad—the trouble was, she was fool enough not to be. Carmichael walked on, making her way toward her Mini. Jones suddenly left the little mingling crowd of family and hurried over to her.

"Thank you. Thank you for your letter, and George, my brother, told me you rang up. That was nice of you." Her eyes looked guarded as she watched Carmichael's face. "I shall be back to work on Monday. I've let them know of course."

Carmichael nodded, but did not speak. Jones nodded back, but did not move, just stood there in the cold sunshine, wanting to say something else, Carmichael thought, but she did not help her.

"You didn't tell me that Mother woke and gave you trouble."

Carmichael looked at her sharply. How did she know? The next sentence told her.

"The sheet, soaking in the basin; I found it, I'm sorry she . . . she did that sometimes." Jones' eyes suddenly welled over with tears.

"Well, she won't do that again." Carmichael's voice was toneless as she answered and then seeing the startled look on Jones' face, amended the sentence by adding, "Poor old thing, it wasn't much of a life for her, or for you. I didn't tell you about her waking; it would only have worried you and anyway I was tired and she was all right then."

She looked at Jones, watchfully. She could see her brother—at least she assumed it was Jones' brother—coming towards them, and Jones performed hasty introductions. Carmichael shook the proffered large, red, rather sticky hand and thought, how different, how very different from Harry's. But she smiled an automatic smile and the man mumbled something and turned away, beckoning to Jones.

"We're having just a little something—you know—a drink and sandwiches. Mother would have wanted it." Jones' words stumbled as she turned to leave Carmichael. "I hoped you'd come—it's at my house. Will you . . . ?" Carmichael shook her head.

"No, I'd better get back," she said briskly and turned to go, longing to get out of it, wishing she hadn't come to the funeral, and yet knowing that it was something she had to do not only as a friend, but also as Nursing Officer; she had felt it was her duty. She had turned her back on Jones when her next question reached her.

"You didn't give her any more pills, did you?"

Carmichael whirled round and looked at Jones. The look was enough. Jones wilted in front of her and said, "I only meant, did you give her anything—did you give her another one as she—as she—"

"Hardly. I'm a nurse too, you know, even if I am an administrator. I would hardly repeat sleeping pills that you'd given—what was it . . . two hours before? Come, Sister Jones." The relapse into formality was obvious and chilly.

"No, no, of course not. Silly of me. I just thought—"

"Well, I should think again," said Carmichael and she walked away, leaving Jones standing there, the brother a short way behind her, looking back impatiently.

Carmichael got into the Mini and banged the door. She sat for a moment. That sheet, of course. But what did it matter? Jones would never dare . . . Anyway, she was out of trouble, rid of that old woman. Carmichael, remembering what the old creature had said to her, about her being flat chested, smiled a little, then shook her head, as if to get rid of an annoying fly. People shouldn't speak to her like that. Oh, no. She'd done a good job; the old woman deserved it. In any case, it was a happy release.

Nothing would come of it; nothing ever did. She put the car into gear, at the same time looking at the mat at her feet.

"I must take these mats out and give the inside of the car a little clean," she said aloud to herself, as she drove the car along the grass-bordered road, round the corner, out of the gate, and back towards the hospital.

During Monday lunchtime Amy Jones and Carmichael met again informally in the rest room. Jones didn't mention her mother until their coffee was nearly finished and they were almost ready to go back to their duties.

"It's so strange," she said. "Now and again, now I'm alone in the house, I hear Mother's stick. When I'm watching television I can hear it—bang, bang, bang. Do you think it will go off, or do you think I'm . . . ?"

Carmichael shook her head. "It's quite natural, you've been looking after her so long, waiting for those thumps on the ceiling; what can you expect?"

Jones nodded and shifted uneasily in her chair. "I almost wish I'd never gone. To the concert I mean. I wish I hadn't. I wish I'd never given her those pills. She always had them, but perhaps . . . When she woke up did she ask for me? They do say, don't they, that sometimes they know—that a last dose . . ."

"What do you mean?" Carmichael's voice was contemptuous. Jones looked up and found the Nursing Officer's eyes fixed on her, the end of Carmichael's sharp nose twitching a little. "What do you mean, a last dose? It's obvious that the last dose before a patient dies must be the last dose."

"I don't know, I don't know," said Jones, miserably. "I mean, if she woke up and I wasn't there to say good-bye to her. And when I saw the bottle in the bathroom when I was clearing up, I thought that—"

"You thought what?"

Jones met Carmichael's cold eyes and tailed off, lamely. "I thought how often I'd given her two and it had been perfectly all right. They suited her . . . they don't give them now, do they? But she's had them for years."

"What were they giving her—to make her sleep, I mean?" Carmichael's voice was calm and detached.

"Oh, Nembutal. They don't give it much now, as you know. But Mother—well, nothing else seemed to work with her, she'd been on Nembutal so long. I thought when I looked at the bottle . . ."

"What did you think?" Carmichael spoke lightly, she was enjoying herself, playing Jones like a salmon.

"Well, I just thought, she won't be wanting any more will she?"

Carmichael came as near as she usually did to a smile, the corners of her mouth going down rather than up. "No, she certainly won't," she said and stood up, looking down at Jones, still with a droop-mouthed smile. "If I were you, I'd take advantage of your freedom now. Get out more, enjoy yourself."

"Yes, I suppose I will, I suppose I must, but I still feel . . . well, I miss her, I suppose."

Carmichael made her way to the door. As she went, she muttered under her breath, "Like a hole in the head you must miss her, my dear."

"What did you say, Miss Carmichael?" Jones asked.

Carmichael turned back and said, "Nothing—nothing at all."

She went through the door of the rest room and started back to her office, still smiling.

CHAPTER 7

Mr. Ealing always gave a party after Christmas, in the first or second week of the New Year. Some of the nursing staff and most of his colleagues were invited. To Carmichael's surprise this year she was included.

She found the card on her desk, asking her to drinks at six-thirty at the Ealing's house. She was slightly startled, not used to this kind of attention. She thought immediately that since she wasn't asked last year or the year before, she supposed it had come to her turn. What would she wear? Her black dress? Yes. She would have to have her hair done. She looked at the date, January 14, and it was already the tenth. She pulled the telephone towards her, asked for an outside line, and dialled the hairdresser.

"Could you do a shampoo and set on the fourteenth? Well, I don't get off till . . . I could make it four-thirty." This was untrue, the party was on a Saturday, Carmichael's day off, but she knew if she had her hair done in the morning and it happened to be a wet or windy day, it would be straight and stringy by the evening. If she had it done as late as possible, she might arrive with it looking . . . She'd let them lacquer it, heavily. All these thoughts flowed through her mind as she spoke. Yes, the hairdresser could do it then. Carmichael put the phone down with a little satisfied bang.

"Good," she said to herself, and Miss Johnson, sitting at her desk at the other end of the room, looked up.

"What's good, Carmichael?"

Carmichael's cheeks tinged with pink. "Oh, nothing really, just making a hair appointment before I go to Mr. Ealing's party." She bridled as she said it, but Johnson confirmed what she had thought.

"Oh, your turn this year, is it? I went last year. I thought it funny asking me, considering I'm not Nursing Officer for his department. It was quite a good party. Decent eats." The remark spoiled a little of Carmichael's pleasure. After all, she was the Nursing Officer in charge of the Eye department. Why had Johnson been asked last year, not her?

She decided to put that matter out of her head and make the most of a rare event—a party—a Consultant's party. She would see to it that Jones knew she was going. After all, there wasn't anyone else to tell, except Tibbles. She smiled to herself. Tibbles wouldn't particularly like it—she didn't like being left in the evening. Not that she often was, but on the rare occasion when Carmichael went out, when she put her coat on and turned the lights off, Tibbles looked quite cross, retired behind the armchair, and gazed out at her, balefully—she was a person, was Tibbles.

The day of the party was clear and dry. Carmichael went out in the morning to do her weekend shopping, to get fish and tinned food for the cat and a cold chicken for herself. She'd just have chicken sandwiches for lunch. She might eat well that night—after all, the odds and ends at a drinks party sometimes made a good meal.

She spent the afternoon getting ready. She couldn't bath after she'd had her hair done—that would court disaster—so during the afternoon she bathed, manicured her nails, put cream on her face, looked in some despair at the red end of her nose. Why was it so red, she wondered? Her hay fever didn't appear in the winter, yet it always seemed to be slightly flushed at the tip.

She decided on her pancake makeup. She'd used it once or twice before—inexpertly. But today she would really try, perhaps even ask the hairdresser's advice. She hung out her black dress in case it should have got creased. It looked nice although she wondered if black was really her colour. Still, it was hardly the time to be wondering now. Pleased as she was to be asked to Mr. Ealing's party, Carmichael didn't really think it was worth buying a new dress—not for that, anyway. There would only be a few nurses and Consultants there, she was sure; no one else she would even know.

However, the first person she saw as she walked into the Ealings' drawing room, which was already fairly full of people, was Emily Maitland. Her heart gave a double lurch. For a moment she wished she'd bought a new frock, in case he was there. Then realized how stupid that was—he couldn't see it. She looked round the room but could not see Harry.

Emily Maitland walked over to someone near Carmichael, obviously not recognizing her, and Carmichael heard her say, "That was a good rubber, wasn't it, last night? I really enjoyed it. I think that little man—what was his name—Jackson?—he's rather good, isn't he? I'd like him again as a partner. Usually I find new partners . . ."

Carmichael at that moment was greeted by Mrs. Ealing, and she moved forward into the crowd, her eyes busily searching for Harry.

After wandering round the room, speaking to no one, a glass in her hand, Carmichael at last came to the conclusion that he was not at the party. The disappointment somehow gave her courage; she had not been ready, not ready to meet him again, not tonight. She walked up and joined the group where Emily Maitland was chatting with three other people.

"Yes, I'm planning on an exhibition—after all, everyone says that my paintings are good, and Jeremy, you know, my young friend," Emily Maitland said, rather archly, "says I really should exhibit in a small gallery in London. Sometimes you have to pay, but it's worth it, and if you can sell one or two . . . Jeremy has approached a gallery for me. I'm waiting to hear from him." The murmurs that greeted this, Carmichael thought, were noncommittal. This was the first time she had realized that Mrs. Maitland painted. Somehow the fact that she was Harry's wife, near the man that Carmichael couldn't get out of her mind, made her want to be near Emily. It was a connection of a sort.

"Is Professor Maitland here tonight?" She came out with the remark almost timidly. Emily Maitland's eyes swept towards her, then away again.

"Oh, no, he hates this kind of thing. Well, not being able to see, what fun is there in it for him? Not that he ever liked parties when he could see. He's a recluse, I sometimes think. He doesn't like small talk."

Carmichael's heart went out to Harry. She hated small talk too—at least, she wasn't capable of indulging in it. Probably he wasn't either and that's why he hated it. She persisted.

"I'm sorry Professor Maitland isn't here. I wanted his advice about something in his field. Medieval stuff I mean." Carmichael was surprised at her own remark.

A man in the group looked towards Emily Maitland. "Oh, anything old—that interests Harry, doesn't it, Emily? You must get in touch with him, telephone him."

Emily Maitland turned away carelessly, as if dismissing her husband from her mind and thinking of more pleasurable things. She walked away to join another group and Carmichael was left standing with the other three people.

"I didn't know Mrs. Maitland painted," she said tentatively and a young man, joining the group at that moment, chimed in.

"Painted! Emily Maitland painting—I'd hardly call it that. Daubing if you like. She thinks it's all right, though, doesn't she, Dad?" He turned to the older man standing beside Carmichael, who frowned rather reprovingly.

"Well, how are we to know, son? I mean these abstracts are beyond me, but maybe there's something in them."

"Not in hers. They're rubbish. It's just Jeremy who helps build the fires of optimism," said the young man, winking at his father. He walked away.

"There's nothing like being sure of yourself. That's my off-spring," said his father, shrugging, and Carmichael, now anxious to glean what information she could spoke again.

"Professor Maitland, does he find his . . . I mean . . . teaching and not able to see . . . does he find . . ."

"No, his blindness doesn't seem to have affected his career. He's a very courageous man. He manages to get there and back to the University every day. True, it's not far, but some people would manage to make a meal of it. He gets there, rain or shine. I must say, his wife isn't very obliging with the car, and she objects to a guide dog. Not that Harry really seems to need one." It was obvious that he didn't like Emily Maitland any more than his son did.

"Has he been blind long?" Carmichael's voice was still tentative, but determined.

"Well, not all that long. About ten or twelve years, I suppose. He went blind about—I should say—ten years after they were married. Terrible luck. He's got some other disease of the eyes— I can't remember what it is. Such a shame, he's such a nice fellow, too."

Carmichael gleaned these pieces of knowledge as if they were little gold nuggets. Suddenly she had a tremendous yearning to see him.

Another half hour went by; Carmichael hardly spoke to anyone. One of the doctors came up to her and said in a friendly way, "Miss Carmichael, isn't it? Did you have a good Christmas?"

She had nodded as enthusiastically as she could. "Yes, lovely," and he'd nodded absently and walked away.

Carmichael felt she couldn't stand and talk animatedly. She couldn't join in the laughter because she didn't know what they were laughing about, and she found it difficult to walk up and join another group. It was only the incentive of finding out more about Harry Maitland that had made her join Emily and her companions.

So she painted. Well, Harry wouldn't be able to see her work, perhaps that was why. And she played bridge—another thing she supposed he wouldn't be able to take part in. Poor Harry! And he was a professor! Her heart swelled with pride. Suddenly she felt she couldn't stand another moment of the party. She would slip away; not thank her hostess, as that would start people saying "Not going are you, already?" She half doubted whether her absence would be noted.

She went upstairs to the bedroom, grabbed her coat, went quietly out of the front door, and got into her car. Once there, she just sat. The old feeling of uncertainty, disgust with herself, and hatred of Emily Maitland, all churned round inside her.

She'd only had one drink, she thought, bitterly; she was certainly fit to drive. Nobody had offered her a second. Maybe they hadn't seen her. But then, Carmichael thought, people don't see me.

CHAPTER 8

Carmichael started the car and drove away towards home. Suddenly, she felt she couldn't go home, couldn't face the flat, not so early. She looked at her watch. It wasn't much after seven-fifteen, pitch dark now, and raining. There was something she wanted to see on television but it didn't come on until eight. Before that, it was a silly comedian and she didn't want that. What should she do until eight? Her heart began to beat faster. She knew what she would do.

She turned the car and drove towards the Maitland house. The street was deserted, wet, dark. She drew up opposite the house and sat there. She was near him—that was something. She presumed he was in, though you couldn't tell, not from the lights. The hall light was on, but that would be for Mrs. Maitland coming home; he wouldn't know whether there was a light on or not.

Again her heart swelled with pity and love. How much, if she dared, she would like to go across, ring the bell, and say, "May I come in and talk? I've been to this beastly party. I didn't like it. I didn't like your wife either. She doesn't seem to care. Does she?" How she would have loved to have said all those things.

Of course, Harry would be loyal and he would immediately answer something like "Oh, Emily, she's all right, she doesn't mean what she says."

Yes, she could imagine that's what he would say, or something like it. You could trust him to say the right thing, the loyal thing, always. How many people could you trust to do that? Few whom Carmichael had met. She sat there, snug in her little car, and looked at the house. She turned off the car lights and sat there in the darkness, warmed by his nearness.

As she sat, preoccupied, aloof, taken completely out of herself

and her own problems, a car drew up, further down the road on
the opposite side. A man got out and closed the door of his car
with an almost furtive softness that made Carmichael watch
him. He looked up and down the road, obviously noting her
parked car, but in the darkness she supposed he presumed it
empty. Looking again up and down the street, he walked to the
house directly opposite her, the Maitlands' house. He opened
the gate, which squeaked slightly, then waited as if he was wondering if the squeak had attracted anyone's attention. Then he
walked up the path. Carmichael quietly wound down her window a couple of inches in order to hear if, when he approached
the door and rang the bell, it was Harry's voice who answered.
But the man did not approach the door; he disappeared round
the side of the house. After a time he came back and Carmichael
suddenly realized he was trying to get into Harry's house, but
not legitimately. The fact that there were no lights except the
hall one probably made him think that everyone was out. Her
heart started to race.

She continued to watch the man, now faintly silhouetted by a
street lamp which was further down the road. She watched him
run his fingers round the casement of the window to the left of
the front door; then, to her horror, after a few seconds he managed to open it. Again he looked round furtively, then opened
the window a little further. Putting one foot on a large stone
that bordered the flower bed, he cocked the other leg easily,
nimbly, over the sill and gently eased himself through. Carmichael saw a gloved hand come out and pull the window to behind him. Then all was darkness and silence again.

Now her mind, as well as her heart, started to race. She
thought, What am I to do? How am I to get Harry out supposing he's in? Oh, God, I've got to do something.

She got out of her car and closed the door as softly as the man
had done, walked quietly across the road, through the open gate,
and up the path. The big, heavy, Tudor-style door confronted
her. A wrought-iron bell hung down, and she prayed it worked.
She looked round the door hastily for a further means of making
Harry hear, but when she pulled on the bell it jangled loudly
inside the house. She thanked God. She felt sick, sick, sick with

apprehension, and in the back of her mind was the feeling, Love does this to you, love does this.

A few seconds only passed, but it seemed to Carmichael like minutes. Then the door opened and Harry stood looking out into the darkness, the hall light behind him. He automatically put out his hand and switched on the porch light—as he must always do, she supposed, for a visitor's benefit, but how vulnerable it makes him.

"Who is it?" he asked.

"It's me, Miss Carmichael, from the hospital. Forgive me, but . . ."

"Emily's all right, isn't she? What's happened?" he asked. Carmichael put out her hand, took his, and spoke softly.

"I was motoring up the street and I saw a man get into your side window. He's in the house now and I thought he might attack you. You wouldn't see him." The grip of his hand tightened on hers.

"I'll go in and ring the police."

"No, no." Carmichael's voice was urgent. "Don't do that. He might be in the room where the phone is. Or anywhere. Upstairs. He might come and attack you. Let me come in with you."

"No, you stop where you are. You can't risk . . ." Carmichael drew him forward urgently, but he resisted her, shaking his head. "No, come with me if you want to, but he's probably more frightened than we are."

He walked determinedly back into the hall, leaving the front door open. Carmichael followed him. She didn't attempt to shut the door; after all, it would be easier if . . . She was afraid, but not for herself. And now she was not as afraid as she had been before; she was with Harry. He was strong, in spite of his blindness, in spite of everything; he was strong and her admiration of him, if possible, increased. They reached the phone.

"Put a light on, please," he said and sat down and dialled the police.

Carmichael looked round her, she stood at the foot of the stairs and listened. The stairs wound round in a semispiral, beautiful, she thought, even in her fear she noticed how lovely the house was. The hall, in which they were, was large, with a parquet floor covered with Indian rugs. Richness.

She wondered what the man, whom she had seen getting through the window, was taking, where he was. Then, they heard a noise. He came out of the door opposite to where Carmichael was standing—paused, assessing the situation; then he pushed passed her and rushed out of the front door. He appeared to be empty-handed, scared, and he didn't know Harry was blind. Carmichael reeled slightly sideways as the man pushed her and Harry looked up from telephoning.

"What was that? Are you all right?"

"Yes, yes, I'm all right. He's gone, out of the front door. I don't think he took anything. At least he hadn't got anything that I could see."

"Well, the police had better come, anyway."

Harry Maitland continued his conversation on the phone and Carmichael went through into the sitting room, noting the open window. She looked through, she heard the car engine further up the road start up, saw the lights come on and the red tail light disappear. They would never catch him, she thought. Automatically, she closed and locked the window, pushing the latch down firmly. She went back into the hall and closed the door.

"Perhaps you shouldn't touch anything—I mean the doorknob, fingerprints," Harry Maitland said.

Carmichael replied immediately, "He was wearing gloves, I saw that when he was getting in through the window."

"You managed to see that he was wearing gloves just passing in your car? You are very observant—you must have got a good look at him. Did you stop when you saw him?"

"Yes." Carmichael could hardly tell him that she had been sitting in her car, opposite his house, just to be near him, but how she longed to do so. "Yes, I did manage to see that," and Harry Maitland put out his hand and she took it automatically and pressed it warmly.

"I can't thank you enough. You've probably saved me from—well, if he'd realized I can't see, he'd probably have hit me over the head. They're charming creatures these days." His voice was

light, but it was obvious to Carmichael that he was shaken.
"Let's go through and have a brandy. I could do with one and
I'm sure you could. I really don't know how to thank you. As I
say, you've probably saved not only the things that might have
been taken but . . ." Carmichael followed him through into the
drawing room.

"Please sit down."

Carmichael sat awkwardly on the soft settee. She did not lean
back. She sat stiffly, but, she realized thankfully, he couldn't see
her. He couldn't see the state her thin, sandy hair had got into
running across the road in the rain. He couldn't see that her
makeup, never very stable, had all gone, from eating the small
things at the party. The little rouge she had put on probably
stood out on her wet cheek. She tried to make up nicely, but it
never lasted. Here it didn't matter, didn't matter at all. She relaxed a little as Harry Maitland handed her a brandy.

"I've put ginger ale in it. I hope that's all right. Or perhaps
you prefer it straight? I like a brandy and ginger ale. Is that all
right?"

She noticed, suddenly, his pallor and rose to her feet and took
his hand again, the hand not holding the glass. "Please sit down.
It has probably shaken you up a bit, more than you realize. Do
sit down."

"Thank you. Not being able to see doesn't help." His voice
was light but underneath Carmichael could sense the tension
and disgust.

"Please, we can't help our disabilities and you seem to handle
yours marvellously." For Carmichael it was an unusual and
tasteful speech and Harry Maitland's face turned to her with
surprise.

"Oh, you know my disabilities. Well, of course you do. You
would. Not being able to see and diabetes put a few restrictions
on me."

"Your wife—I met her at the Ealing party. I was there and
talked to her."

Harry Maitland put his glass down on the table and put his
hand on the watch on his wrist. "It's only eight o'clock. You
must have come away early. Emily won't be home yet. She'll

stay till the bitter end. Why did you come away? Didn't you like it?"

"No, I'm not very good at parties. I didn't like it very much, though it was kind of them to ask me, but I decided to go back to my flat and talk to my cat." Again it was a very un-Carmichael-like speech and Harry Maitland smiled.

"Good company, cats. I wish we could have one, but Emily doesn't like them."

At that moment, the bell rang. Carmichael got up as if to assist Harry, then realized that he didn't need her help. He crossed the room, went out the door, into the hall. She heard the murmur of voices; then the front door shut, and two policemen entered the room with Harry Maitland. They sat down, one getting out a notebook, and started to ask both of them what had happened.

"I think this young lady, Miss Carmichael, saved me from a nasty accident."

The policeman nodded. "Do you think he took anything, sir?"

"I don't know, I shall have to wait till my wife comes in. He may have taken some small things from the tables round about. I wouldn't know and Miss Carmichael doesn't know our house. It was just lucky that she was passing."

"Lucky you were so observant, miss, just driving past."

Carmichael had to put this right. "Well, when I saw him getting out of the car and going up the garden path, I thought he looked furtive, and I knew it was Professor Maitland's house. So when I saw him go round to the side, I stopped, switched off my lights, and waited."

"Lucky you did, miss, very lucky. They can be vicious. He could have hit out at you, sir, being—" He paused, embarrassed, and Harry Maitland helped him out.

"With my being blind, you mean? Yes, indeed, he could have crept up on me and he was pretty silent. My hearing is good, but I didn't hear him get in. He could have coshed me all right—I was in the kitchen and of course I didn't know . . ."

"Right, sir. When your wife gets back, perhaps you'll ask her if she'll be kind enough to look round to see if there's anything missing and let us know. We shall probably want to see you at the station, if you don't mind."

Harry Maitland smiled. "No, I don't mind, if you want any more information, of course I'm at your disposal, and I'm sure Miss Carmichael, if you wish . . ." He looked towards her.

"Of course, anything more I can remember."

"That window, sir, needs looking at, if he could get it open so easily."

"It does. It's got a screw lock on it and I should have made sure. I don't always though, but in future you can be sure I will."

"Well, thank you, sir and miss, that will be all for the moment."

Harry Maitland nodded and smiled. He accompanied them to the door, closed it behind them, and came back. He sank down on the settee beside Carmichael.

He looked tired and Carmichael ventured, "Can I get you another brandy?"

He nodded. "Just a small one. My doctor doesn't like me to have too much, but I think tonight is a bit of an exception, don't you?"

Carmichael's heart seemed to be singing. She was doing something for him, doing something he didn't mind about. He was such an independent man, but felt now, probably from the shock of what had happened, he didn't mind having someone do something for him, if only just to pour him a drink. She crossed the room to the bar cart, poured a brandy, added the dry ginger, and took it back to him.

How she longed to touch his hand. She held the glass out in the hope that his fingers would brush hers as he took the glass. They did—the touch was like an electric shock to her. She would have given almost anything to have taken his hand in hers and cradle it, hold it firmly as she had at the doorway. Now, they were relaxed, they were alone, they were together, sitting in this beautiful, spacious room, on the soft settee. How she would have loved to have taken him in her arms and say, "Don't worry, I know what it's like for you."

But of course she couldn't and she didn't. Instead she said, "Well, all's well that ends well, Professor Maitland."

"Thanks to you, Miss Carmichael." Harry Maitland took a sip of his brandy and looked at her with his sightless eyes. Carmichael gazed back at him. She loved him more than she had loved anyone or anything in her whole life and it was a terrible and desperate feeling.

The sound of the key turning in the lock of the front door caused Harry Maitland to rise to his feet and put his glass down on the table.

"That will be Emily," he said.

It was Emily. She came across the hall, briskly, and stood in the doorway, looking at the two of them, eyebrows raised high on her forehead in an expression of astonishment and slight amusement, Carmichael thought.

"What are you doing here, Sister Carmichael?" she asked.

Carmichael winced, she wasn't a Sister; she was Miss Carmichael. She felt the remark might be deliberate, but Harry broke in before she could answer.

"I've had rather a nasty experience, and if it hadn't been for Miss Carmichael here, I don't know what would have happened."

"A nasty experience?" Emily came forward into the room and looked at the brandy glasses. "An experience from which you needed to be resuscitated, both of you, obviously," she said lightly, but Harry Maitland broke in again, more firmly, and told her briefly what had happened.

"Well, that was a nice thing . . . he might have taken anything . . . did he?"

"I don't know, Emily. We were waiting for you to come home to see. He was only in this downstairs room. Miss Carmichael came so quickly that he was frightened—she rang the doorbell, came in, and he just dashed across the hall and out of the front door. Miss Carmichael said that as far as she could see he was not carrying anything, but he could have put something small in his pocket. That's why I want you to look round and see if anything is missing."

"My patch boxes!" Emily Maitland walked quickly over to a

small table and looked hurriedly at the array of enamel boxes. "No, they seem to be all here. Thank goodness. How did he get in?"

Harry Maitland motioned with his hand toward the window.

"You must have left it open," Emily said. "As you can't see, at least you should pull the catch firmly and screw it down. You could feel whether it is closed."

Carmichael felt her colour mounting. To speak like that to him, in front of her, without any affectionate concern, thinking only of her precious boxes! Emily slipped off her mink coat and threw it over the back of the settee where the two had been sitting and sank into an armchair.

"Well, after that news, perhaps I'd better have a brandy too," she said. Harry got up immediately. Carmichael half rose to help him and Emily stopped her. "Harry's perfectly capable of getting me a drink, you know. It's just that he's not capable of shutting windows."

Carmichael felt a bitter taste well up into her mouth as if she was going to be sick. Perhaps it was the brandy, perhaps it was hate.

She answered, tartly, "Professor Maitland has had rather a nasty shock and I believe it might make him feel . . ."

"Oh, his state of health. You've been hearing about all his troubles, have you? His diabetes, his eyes—there's no end to it, is there?"

It became apparent to Carmichael that Emily Maitland had had quite enough to drink and was irritated by the fact that she, Carmichael, was there and consequently she was unable to relax properly as she would have liked to do. Carmichael looked at her watch.

"Well, I'd better be going."

"Oh, please don't hurry on my account," said Emily, taking the brandy from Harry's hand. "Please don't hurry. You've obviously done something we should be very grateful for. If my Battersea boxes had disappeared—they're impossible to find now and worth—"

"Well, I've often told you they should be in a case, not displayed like that on a table, dear," said Harry Maitland, mildly.

She shrugged her shoulders. "I like them like that, and if the window is properly shut and locked, they would be all right . . . How did you manage to see, just driving past, that a man was getting through our window?" She gazed at Carmichael curiously.

"I thought he looked furtive and I slowed the car down." Carmichael felt uncomfortable.

"I see." Emily Maitland looked at her, with a slight smile on her face. Did she guess? Carmichael couldn't be sure. The next question was even more disconcerting.

"Where do you live?" Carmichael told her her address.

"And you were at the Ealing's weren't you. Did you leave early? I didn't notice."

Carmichael nodded. She could see the conclusion Emily Maitland was drawing. It was, "If you came from the Ealings' and you live . . . How was it you were driving past here?" Carmichael lied.

"I was going to call in to see a friend, whose house wasn't far from the Ealings'."

It didn't quite fit, but she prayed Emily Maitland wouldn't notice. Whether she did or not was hard to know. Her hard, pebblelike brown eyes stayed fixed on Carmichael's face; the little smile persisted round her lips. Then she seemed to lose interest, sipped her brandy, and nodded.

"I see, you just happened to be passing. How very, very lucky."

Harry Maitland suddenly rose. "I think I'll go to my room, Emily. I feel a bit tired."

"That's probably due to the brandy, dear. I don't know how much you've had. I thought the doctor said—"

"Oh, I haven't had much, Emily, don't worry."

He went towards the door and Carmichael resisted the temptation to get up, realizing that what she physically longed for was another touch of his hand. As if he felt her wish, he suddenly turned and held out his hand to her and she hastily walked after him and clasped it.

"Thank you again. I'll never be able to thank you enough for this evening. We'll be in touch, won't we, Emily?"

His wife did not answer, but just watched him leave the room. As he passed through the door, he wavered slightly to his left and put his hand out to touch the door frame. Then, to Carmichael's surprise, she heard him, not going upstairs, but walking across the hall, opening a door opposite the drawing room door and closing it behind him.

"He doesn't go upstairs. He has a special little annexe down here; because of his heart, you know—then he doesn't have to use the stairs."

Carmichael could not understand the smile on Emily's face, but she determined tomorrow, as soon as she could, to read Harry's notes, to see just exactly what his heart condition was, to learn more about his illness. Poor Harry, hadn't he enough to cope with with his diabetes and his blindness?

"I must go." Carmichael picked up her coat, shrugged it on, and turned again to meet the gaze of Emily Maitland's hard eyes.

"Nurses. I suppose they become nurses because they like looking after people—is that right?"

Carmichael couldn't see why Emily had made this remark. She nodded.

"I suppose so."

"I would never have made a nurse, neither have I ever felt the slightest desire to look after anyone. I like to be looked after." She met Carmichael's stare and then lowered her eyes.

"Thank you for tonight, though. It was good of you to look after him. I still don't know how you managed to be outside the house, but it was lucky you were."

"I'm glad I was able to help." It sounded lame, but that was how Emily Maitland made Carmichael feel.

Emily accompanied her to the door, threw it wide open. They both looked about them into the dark garden.

"I just hope he doesn't come back, but I shall certainly see that the windows are secured." Emily smiled and Carmichael tried to smile back, but felt herself fail. "Where's your car, then?"

"Over there on the other side of the road."

"Neatly parked, considering it was done in an emergency."

"What do you mean?" Carmichael turned her head sharply

and looked directly at Emily. The face that confronted her appeared innocent, open and the mouth was still smiling.

"Just what I said. What else could I mean?" Emily Maitland turned and went in and shut the door firmly behind Carmichael, who made her way across to her car.

As she opened the door and got in, she realized that the keys were still in the ignition. The car could have been stolen; still, it hadn't been. As the courtesy light revealed the cosy interior, she felt years had passed since she was last in the car; instead it had hardly been more than an hour. She got in, slammed the door, started the engine, switched on her lights, and drove away, her mind in a turmoil—not her usual feeling of inadequacy, but one of terrible, destroying frustration.

CHAPTER 9

The next day seemed endless. The administrative work that Carmichael usually found interesting seemed to drag and be dull and boring. At lunch she was so silent that Jones' volubility dried up in the face of Carmichael's preoccupation.

At ten past five Carmichael walked down to the Records department. She tried the door, tentatively, to see if it was locked and to make sure that the Records clerks had all gone home—not that she expected anyone would stay late, she thought, with a little curl of her lips. No, they were clock watchers, they went home as soon as they possibly could. Indeed, she had often found them getting into their coats or powdering their noses at five minutes to five. Sometimes she would glance at the clock and then at them, meaningly, but it made no difference. In any case, it was nothing to do with her. She was in charge of the nursing, not the Records, side of the hospital and they would have been quick to point this out to her if she had made her rebuke more apparent.

Carmichael fetched the keys from the secretary's office, noting that he'd gone home, too. She was glad to have the office to herself. She turned the key in the door behind her; she did not want to be disturbed. She went to the filing cabinet that would tell her Harry Maitland's number, found it, and then travelling her finger along the rows and rows of folders, eventually came to the name, MAITLAND, HAROLD.

As she drew the folder out, she felt an almost sensual pleasure in handling the notes which belonged to him, which were about him. She took them to a desk, sat down, and started to read. Yes, he had been admitted to the ward for the stabilisation of his diabetes, twice—to the Private Ward. She wondered again, momentarily, why he had not seen Mr. Ealing as a private patient, then remembered that Ealing did not take private patients. Yes, he had been under the physician privately, but only for his diabetes. She went carefully through the notes, but could find no reference at all to heart disease. Strange. She couldn't understand Emily's explanation of the downstairs room. Was it possible that he'd been somewhere since about his heart—perhaps to a London consultant? But even then there would be some letter referring to it in his notes and she could find nothing. There was one letter from Harry's own general practitioner to Mr. Ealing, dated some two years previously. That particular letter pleased her. It read:

Dear Gerald,

This courageous man, whose diabetic retinitis I'm afraid precludes him from any kind of operation for his cataract, has asked if he might see you for a further opinion. I have, of course, agreed. I know you will help him in any way you can. He has, as you know, already seen Sir Cholmondeley Bligh in London and was told by him that nothing more can be done. However, he wishes to try again. If there were any question of an operation, I know he would be delighted, but having read your first opinion, I doubt this.

He has made himself independent and carries on his position as lecturer in Medieval History at the University, and as far as he's able, I gather, leads a perfectly normal life.

I feel the domestic situation is not quite all it should be. His wife, an energetic and outgoing woman, is a little irked by the restrictions caused by her husband's disability and of course, by his diabetes—hence his anxiety to do all he can about his sight.

I hope I'm not troubling you in asking you to see Professor Maitland again.

Thank you for doing so.

That letter confirmed what Carmichael already knew: Emily Maitland was not a caring person. All she thought about was herself, her painting, her bridge, her cocktail parties. Carmichael slammed the notes shut; then felt as if she had hurt Harry by doing so. She opened them again, closed them gently, slipped them into the correct place, and left the Records office. She almost wished she could take the notes home with her, to read again and again. This, of course, was impossible and, anyway, ridiculous, but she knew enough about him now to realize that his blindness was permanent. She was still puzzled that the heart condition was not mentioned anywhere in the notes.

When Carmichael arrived home she went about her usual chores, still thinking of Harry, getting herself some supper, feeding Tibbles—her heart, light. She felt that she was experiencing something that other women experienced, and she realized now what it was that made them act as they sometimes did —she felt at one with women in love. Every now and again she admonished herself, tried to bring herself back to reality by saying, What good is it? But that didn't matter. The very thought that he was there, in the same world, sitting, perhaps, on that settee, or perhaps gone to bed early because last night had made him . . . She wondered, should she ring up to see how he was? Yes, she would, but she'd better leave it a little. Somehow she would manage to see him again.

The next evening, back again from the hospital, a little later because she had wanted to do some extra work in her office, she was again going through her little routine—preparing supper and a meal for Tibbles. Tibbles had just mewed to be let in and now followed Carmichael across the sitting room and into the kitchen, Carmichael talking constantly to her, as she did—it did away with loneliness and she thought the cat understood. In the quiet of the night she had told Tibbles all about Harry, the cat lying at the foot of her bed, the silhouette of her head, ears pricked, against the lighted window.

There was a knock on the flat door. Carmichael was expecting no one. Jones was on duty till eight-thirty. She hastily dried her hands on the kitchen towel, patted her hair, and opened the door. She could hardly believe her eyes—she felt her knees go weak, she felt almost afraid they would let her down, she was trembling—it was Harry Maitland.

"I hope this is the right flat? I did ask someone on the stairs— it is Miss Carmichael?" he asked and held out his hand as he always did in an unfamiliar place and Carmichael took it and held it firmly in her own.

She was not thinking; thought had gone from her for the moment. A glorious feeling swelled over her. She wanted, longed to say "Yes, it's me, my darling" and put her arms round him.

Instead, she said stiffly, "Oh, Professor Maitland, do come in." She drew him forward, he came in hesitantly, and she closed the door behind him.

"I've brought you these. I wanted to say thank you again." He held out a sheaf of yellow roses he had been holding down by his side. She took them, very near to tears. No man had ever bought her flowers before, no man ever. She took the roses in her arms and cradled them like a baby.

"They're beautiful, but you shouldn't have—really you shouldn't have."

"Why shouldn't I?" In her oversensitive state Carmichael thought that perhaps he thought the remark silly; everyone said "You shouldn't have." It was stupid, common, probably not what he was used to.

"Please come through," she said. Again she took his hand and led him through into the sitting room, helped him into an armchair by the fire, took the white stick he carried and placed it against the side of the fireplace, carefully. The moment was full of self-consciousness, of doubt, which seemed to communicate itself to Harold Maitland for he said, "Perhaps I've come at the wrong time, I'm sorry if I've interrupted anything."

He looked round, vaguely, as if trying to sense if there was anything going on in the room that he had interrupted. Carmichael was about to reply when Tibbles solved everything for her by jumping up onto Harry's knee and purring loudly. A look of pleasure spread over his face. He stroked the cat's head.

"A cat. I'd forgotten you have a cat. You did tell me last night —no, not last night; it was the night before, wasn't it, but I'd forgotten." Tibbles curled herself up on his knees and he leaned back, relaxing in the armchair, still stroking the cat. The cat rubbed its mouth against his hand. "They do that, you know. There's a little gland in their mouth—it marks out their terri-

tory; that's why they do it. I like to think it's affection, though,"
he said and his voice, too, was relaxed.

Carmichael felt thankful, very thankful for Tibbles, who
knew how to behave socially even if she didn't.

"She likes you, obviously. I didn't know about the little gland
in their mouths—she's always doing it." Carmichael could have
bitten her tongue out. "She's always doing it"—that detracted
from the fact that the cat was affectionate towards him. Oh,
God, why can't I say the right thing, she thought.

"I'll put these in water. Would you like a cup of tea?" He
shook his head, smiling. "Of course you wouldn't," she said. "A
cup of tea! What am I thinking of! It's seven o'clock. Will you
have a sherry?" Afraid he was about to shake his head again, she
ended it with "Please."

Perhaps Harry Maitland felt the pleading in it and sensed the
loneliness in her, for he answered, "Thank you—if you will tell
me exactly where it is so that I won't knock it all over your
carpet."

It was said in a jocular manner to make her feel better, she
was sure. She fetched the sherry from the kitchen and poured
two glasses, stood one on the table, and placed the other in his
hand. She put a small table beside him, telling him exactly
where it was. He nodded, but did not put the glass down.

"How did you get here . . . I mean, how did you know
where I lived?"

"I rang the hospital—that was easy. Then I got a taxi from the
University straight here."

"You haven't kept it waiting?"

"No, no, I sent it away. I can ring for another from here."

"Oh, how nice it is—it's so nice to see you . . . I wasn't expecting—"

"Me?" he asked.

"No, no. I wasn't expecting these lovely roses. They're so
beautiful. Why did you . . . ? I mean, there was no need and
yet I'm so glad." Carmichael was getting lost in a maze of words.
The things she wanted to say, beautifully, correctly, in the manner in which he was used to from other people. She was afraid,
terrified that she would say something which sounded ill bred.

"Of course I should. I shan't forget it. It was a very terrifying experience, and if it hadn't been for you . . . I think roses are a poor enough reward. We must do something more for you. Emily agrees. We would like to take you out to dinner one night."

"Oh, yes, thank you, I would really like that. It's not only the roses—it's your coming here. I mean . . ."

Harry looked up. Was there surprise on his face? It was difficult to tell. He sipped his sherry.

"It's a good sherry. You've got good taste in sherry," he said.

Carmichael was just about to say that it had been given to her by one of the consultants, but she stopped herself in time and merely said, "I'm glad you like it," and thanked God for the Consultant who hadn't given her a cheap sherry but a good one.

Every moment that was flying by while he was sitting in her chair, the cat purring cosily on his lap, was as precious to her as diamonds.

"I can feel the heat of a fire on my legs. It's an electric fire, is it not?"

"Yes, it's one of those with the log effect. You know, flames—or rather, pretend flames. I don't think I could cope with carrying coal up here and the flames do make a little movement in the room." Carmichael said this without thinking and Harry turned to her again, sympathy if not sight in his eyes.

"Yes, it could get lonely, I would imagine, when you live on your own," he said.

Carmichael didn't like that. She felt he shouldn't know that she was lonely. She would like him to think that she was in demand, always out and about. Well, at least he knew that she'd been at the Ealing cocktail party, but then, she had told him that she didn't like parties, so she wasn't quite sure how to handle the next remark and bungled it.

"Oh, I'm not lonely. I quite like being by myself. I like—"

"Well, I won't stay long," Harry Maitland said, humorously, and again Carmichael hated herself for not having the expertise to handle the small talk, for continually making gaffes.

"Oh, I didn't mean—," she began.

"I know you didn't," Harry Maitland's voice had a pleasing, laughing quality that was new to her. "But I really must go." He put the glass down carefully on the table beside him, feeling with one hand to make sure that it was safely placed, then rose to his feet. The cat had jumped down and was rubbing herself against his trousers, still purring. He bent down and stroked her side.

"I wish you were mine, cat, or one like you." He straightened himself, still smiling, looking in the direction in which Carmichael stood.

"Will you ring for a taxi for me?"

"Of course. Are you sure I can't run you back in the Mini? I mean, it's not far."

He shook his head. "No, I won't have that; most certainly not."

Carmichael, with difficulty, relinquished the hope of having a little more time with him, went to the phone, and dialled the taxi number. They both stood. Carmichael knew the taxi rank was only five minutes away; she didn't know whether to ask him to sit down again or not. She stood, twisting her hands together, trying to think of something memorable to say that would make him go away remembering her, but nothing would come.

"She's taken to you. Tibbles, I mean."

"Yes, she appears to have. I'm glad; they're very discerning animals, cats." Again his voice was humorous, jocular.

Carmichael began to wonder if perhaps this was the tone he felt he must take with her, that that was all she was worth. Then she tried to dismiss the thought, searching frantically again for something to say, but before she could speak, there was a brief hoot from the street below and she crossed over to the window and looked down.

"Your taxi," she said. "I hoped—they would take longer." What an effort it was to say those words. Harry turned to her and there was a pleasant smile on his face. It was hard to say what he thought of the remark.

"Thank you. Thank you for ringing and thank you for the sherry. May I ask you to see me downstairs? I don't want to fall from top to bottom—that would be very embarrassing." Carmichael put her hand gently on his elbow and guided him out.

"Stairs now," she said. She felt better in this role. The nurse in me, she thought; at least with that I can help him. They walked down the stairs, across the hall to the front door, and down the few steps. Harry turned round and held out his hand.

"Good night, Professor Maitland," Carmichael said, and Harry smiled.

"I think we might make it Harry now, particularly if we're going out to dinner together. Easier, don't you think? And if I may call you—?"

"Agnes," Carmichael said. She hated the name. Harry nodded. "Thank you for the roses and thank you for coming. It must have been such an effort to find the flat and everything."

He was about to step into the taxi, but turned to her. "Not all that much of an effort, you know. I do get around to other universities to lecture. I'm not that helpless."

It was said with a smile, but Carmichael immediately knew she had irritated him. He got into the taxi and the taxi man slammed the door behind him and went round and got into the driver's seat. Harry raised a hand. He said something but the window was shut and Carmichael couldn't hear what it was.

The taxi drove away, and Carmichael felt as if her heart was going with it. There was nothing left now. She went in out of the cold night, shut the front door, went upstairs to her flat, and closed that door, leaning a moment against it. Then, rather to her surprise, her spirits began to rise.

Tibbles greeted her with enthusiasm. Mechanically, Carmichael went into the kitchen, put some more food into a saucer, and put it down for the cat, who began to eat greedily. Carmichael watched. Oh, to be a cat, she thought, not having to worry about how you behaved—indeed, Tibbles had behaved beautifully, sat on Harry's lap, purred, and made a very good impression; perhaps I did too.

The lightening of her spirits continued. She prepared her supper, took it to the sitting room on a tray, and switched on the television. She had decided not to think about his visit. Not yet; because she was sure she would find great gaps and hollows where she had failed—she knew herself so well. She fought off the thought of it and just gazed at the roses, took in their perfume, and sat thinking, He brought them, Harry brought them for me. Thinking about the whole visit—that she must put off till later, when she was in bed, in the dark.

Supper over, she took the tray out into the kitchen and, divorced from the picture on the television, she began to think; she couldn't wait, not till bedtime. She had got to think, think of the visit, go over it minute by minute. She went back, switched the picture off, sat down, and gazed into the electric flames circling in front of her. Each tiny morsel of conversation she wanted to bring back.

The sherry, that had been a bonus. It was a good thing she had had a decent sherry to offer him. But then, that remark about being lonely and by herself . . . Oh, God. She buried her face in her hands. That had been awful. Other things came back to her. She had used the words "lovely" and "beautiful"—she knew she had and she was sure people didn't. They didn't say "lovely" all the time, or "beautiful," but she had. Nervousness had made her repeat the words more and more, she was sure. What had she called "lovely," "beautiful"? The roses? The fact that he had come to see her? She couldn't remember, but she felt the words were awful—it was like saying "Pleased to meet you." At least she hadn't said that.

Then, the awful business about the taxi. She'd acted as if he were confined to his house—not a clever, professional man, a professor who went all over the place and lectured, probably abroad. Yes, she'd acted as if she thought she had to . . . that she would have to see him home. She was mad, mad to have said that, to have offered even. And anyway, that was the last thing Harry would have liked; he was independent—she knew that much about him. She remembered with horror that she had almost tried to put him into the taxi, like an invalid, like she would a patient.

Emily, his wife, was right: a hard attitude was probably what he liked; it bolstered up his self-confidence. Emily probably jabbed the insulin in every day and that was it; after that, she wasn't interested in his problems. Yes, Harry probably liked it like that. What a mess she'd made of it! And yet, she thought dully, what does it matter?

The dinner. She'd go, of course. She couldn't resist the

thought of being close to him. She decided that tomorrow at the hospital she'd read his notes again, just to have the joy of handling them. She went into the bedroom and sat down in front of the dressing table mirror and studied her face.

"You're getting ridiculous," she said aloud. "What, in God's name, are you thinking about? Look at your face, your hair, everything about you."

It was all no good. Carmichael prepared for bed, took Tibbles down to the front door; the cat went out immediately into the garden. Carmichael stood there, looking out into the night, her mind a blank now. She didn't want to think. After about ten minutes the cat came in, tail erect, and rushed up the stairs. Carmichael followed her, slowly.

A depression came over her, so deep that it surprised even herself. It was like being in the middle of a black cloud. But then, she tried to relieve it by thinking, he had come to see her— he had brought her roses.

CHAPTER 10

Next day Carmichael arrived at her office and greeted Miss Johnson, who was already seated at her desk, neat, efficient, good-looking.

"Had a night out, old girl? You look a bit rough," she said, kindly, but Carmichael took it ill.

"That's a nice way to be greeted," she said testily.

"Oh, sorry. I didn't realize I'd put my foot in it. Thought you might have a hangover, been to a party, or something. After all, old Ealing isn't the only one who gives parties, you know. I don't know what you get up to at night, Carmichael." Johnson bent down again to the off duty rotas that she was checking.

She went on, as if to change the subject. "I don't know what the hell that Sister on Men's Surgical does with her rotas. She's got three nurses on there and five off. I'll have to go and see her." She got up. "Sorry again if I've put my foot in it. I didn't mean to." She added, eyeing Carmichael with amusement.

Carmichael looked up, deciding to lie, let Johnson think she had been out. "It's all right. As a matter of fact, I was out on a bit of a party last night. Perhaps I indulged too freely. Not necessarily with the drink, I mean, but with the food, too; it was very good." She looked at Johnson, challengingly, but Johnson seemed to take the remark as being perfectly natural.

She shrugged and smiled. "Jolly good. I think it's nice when we older ones get asked to parties and not all the young, good-looking brats. I sometimes envy them." This was said with good humour and genially, but again Carmichael took it amiss.

"We're not that old, for goodness' sake," she said. Johnson pretended to cringe.

"Sorry, I've done it again, haven't I? Well, I'll go down and vent my spleen on Sister Carter. You know what she's like—if she finds she's short-staffed, she's up here, knocking on my door, expecting me to do something about it and I can see her saying to herself, 'That's what she's paid for, she's an administrator.' " She waved a piece of paper in her hand. "We'll have some coffee when I get back. That will make you feel better." She beat a hasty retreat, closing the door none too softly after her.

Carmichael put her head in her hands. Her eyes felt hot and stinging. She supposed that was lack of sleep. About a hundred times she'd gone through the interchange between Harry and herself, almost wishing at times that he hadn't called, then hating herself for even thinking of that. If this was what people called being in love, for the fiftieth time she thought how much it hurt. Harry was unavailable—he was married; she, she looked like she did—rough, as Johnson had put it. Not that he could see her but . . .

"Get on with your work," she muttered to herself and she pulled a pile of papers towards her—Nursing Procedures—ready to check. It was a relief to have something concrete to do, something on which she had to concentrate.

The morning crept by. She did the round of the wards and departments. In Out Patients they were particularly busy—it was the Orthopaedic Clinic and, as usual, Sister was loud in her complaints: the Surgeon was late and the patients were getting restless. Carmichael listened and said that she would have a word with the culprit when she got the chance. She knew she wouldn't; it was difficult for a Nursing Officer to criticise a Consultant. In private she did, but in public Carmichael could only point out in rather acid tones, that the Clinic was late. She could not directly accuse the Surgeon of being tardy at his Clinic.

"I expect he's seeing a private patient—that's why he's bloody well late," said the Out Patients Sister. "Yes, nurse?" She looked up as a nurse approached her.

"The sterile supplies haven't been delivered, Sister, and I need things—to stock the Clinic with—I need some more syringes and . . ."

"Oh, God, that's all we need. Why haven't they come, do you know, Miss Carmichael? It's getting later and later . . . that bloody porter comes later with them every morning. What is it? It's half past ten, for God's sake, and they're supposed to be delivered at nine." Carmichael nodded.

"I'll see to it," she said abruptly and walked out of the department, glad that she'd got a reason, a valid reason, for telling somebody off.

The Out Patients Sister looked after her with some appreciation and Carmichael heard her say to the nurse beside her, "There's one thing about old Carmichael, she used to be an Out Patients Sister and she's sympathetic. She really gets things done. I don't like her much, but she's useful when it comes to something like this."

The nurse went off, muttering to herself, and Carmichael smiled and walked out of the door that led back to the hospital.

Next day Carmichael felt better. She was beginning to pick up the good things of Harry's visit which still occupied the larger part of her thinking. In the middle of the morning her phone rang. It had been silent for some time and the ringing made her jump. She got plenty of phone calls—ward Sisters complaining of staff shortages, that the linen hadn't come, or that they'd no cleaner, plenty of things—but this morning had been quiet. She picked up the phone and found that it was an outside call.

Carmichael waited while she was put through, her heart beginning to beat rapidly. She put her hand on her chest and raised her eyes and saw Johnson watching her. It was hateful at times, sharing an office with someone. If only she could have a bit of privacy. Then she remembered that when she'd first got this job she'd been rather pleased she'd been sharing it with someone; but not now. She waited. It seemed ages before she heard the click and the telephonist put the call through to her. It was Emily Maitland.

"Miss Carmichael? Oh, good. I said 'Sister Carmichael' and they corrected me. Sorry about that. It's this dinner engagement that Harry wants—well, I want it too, of course. Where would you like to go? Anywhere particular? And when?"

There was a pause, a dead silence. Carmichael felt frozen; she didn't know how to cope with this woman. So self-assured—Carmichael had the feeling that Emily Maitland would be good at everything or behave as if she was.

"Would you prefer during the week or at the weekend?" Carmichael finally asked, clearing her throat, her voice husky with nerves.

"I'm asking you," said Emily. "I don't mind. In the week. Would you rather go out to dinner after you've been to work or when you've been off all day? That's what Harry wants to know and I'm just asking."

"How about Saturday evening—would that do?" Carmichael said tentatively and Emily's voice came back, slightly obliterated by the rustle of paper of her diary, thought Carmichael.

"As a matter of fact, Saturday is rather good. I usually play bridge on Saturday nights, but one of our four has been taken ill and another one has got a crashing cold. So yes, that would be fine. Shall we say seven o'clock here? You know where the house is."

Was it said with a sarcastic smile? Carmichael wondered. She replied as evenly as she could. "Yes, seven o'clock will be perfect. I'll be there."

"You can park your car in our drive. There's plenty of room. Where would you like to go? Where do you usually go? Where do you think is good?"

Carmichael's mind was quite definitely blank. She hadn't been out to dinner, hadn't been to any of the local places, except a small café or two with Jones.

"Oh, I'd rather you chose somewhere. I'm sure you know . . ."

Emily broke in again, briskly. "All right. We'll arrange to go to that roadhouse at Yatford, Rosebarn. It's quite nice. Quite a drive, but I don't mind driving and Harry likes it there, too. It's better that he goes somewhere he's used to."

"Yes, yes, that's fine, that's lovely. Seven o'clock on Saturday. Yes, all right, thank you." She put the phone down and wondered immediately if she should have said thank you. Did it sound servile? Oh Lord, did she have to think of everything she said? The dinner engagement was going to be pretty awful if she thought that way. She'd end up by dreading it instead of looking forward to being near Harry, even with Emily there, for a whole evening.

"Oh, another date, eh? Living it up, aren't we?" said Johnson, but this time Carmichael did not reply testily.

She smiled. "Yes, it's a date. We're going to . . ." and she named the restaurant at Yatford, and Johnson's eyebrows shot up.

"M-m, pricey. He must be rich, lucky old you," she said. "That's not the sort of place you go dutch with a man." Carmichael looked at her, a slight feeling of superiority coming over her after all . . .

"I don't think I'd go dutch with anyone, not a man anyway," she said and Johnson smiled.

"I would, if he were handsome enough and nice enough. Have done." She bent down again and went on writing.

Carmichael didn't answer; she thought the less she said to Johnson the better. In a way, now, she was glad Johnson had been there when the phone went. Had it been Harry . . . well, thank goodness she hadn't said "Mrs. Maitland"—that would have dispelled any suspicions on Johnson's part that she was going out with a man; that would have been a pity. That had been clever, she thought, but that mood passed quickly when she realized she hadn't done it with Johnson in mind. She had just happened not to say "Mrs. Maitland."

With an air of importance she bent down to the side of her desk, picked up her handbag, took out her diary, and made the entry. The whole week was blank, except Saturday . . . As she wrote it down it seemed an age away, but actually it was only three days. She had time to—yes, she really would have to get a new frock this time. She'd get some really nice perfume, too. Harry might not be able to see the dress, but he could smell the perfume. She looked across at Miss Johnson.

"Do you use perfume?" she asked.

"Yes, I do. When I can afford it. I like Chanel No. 5. When we got our rise last year, I bought myself a small bottle. Why? Thinking of Saturday?"

Carmichael didn't answer. She bent again to the task on her

desk, but she could feel Johnson's eyes still fixed on her searchingly. She made an excuse, got up, said she was going to Out Patients to see if their sterile supplies had come. When she got outside the door she found she was still trembling.

Actually, she did not go towards the Out Patients department, but to the Children's Ward. She longed to tell someone and the only one she could tell was Jones. When she reached the Children's Ward and pushed open the door she saw the paediatrician was doing a round with Sister, so she withdrew and after a suitable wait in the corridor went back to her office. Perhaps, she thought, it was better. Keep your own counsel and say nothing—it was lonely, but wise. Forgetting all about Out Patients and its delivery of sterile supplies, forgetting everything but Saturday, she made her way back up the stairs.

The dress. That was Carmichael's next problem, and quite a problem. If only—if only they were going out alone, she driving him to this hotel or whatever it was, just the two of them in the Mini, how lovely that would be. Of course, he wouldn't be able to see her, wouldn't even know what she had on. Because of that, she decided that whatever she chose had to feel silky, just in case he touched her or brushed against her. Then there was the perfume.

In the dress shop, standing in front of the mirror in the small cubicle, Carmichael took private stock of herself. She was appalled at the price of the dress. It was pale green and felt beautiful to the touch. She was glad the saleswoman had left her alone to think about it. She swirled round a little. The dress swept smoothly against her thighs. Her waist was small, her breasts were flat but fashionable. The collar of the dress was quite high, which was good, because Carmichael didn't like her neck—it always looked sallow to her, like her face. She wondered if green was right for her, then decided: yes.

She'd get her hair done the day of the dinner, of course; taking her jumper off to try this dress on had made it stand out, spikily. It was fine, like a baby's. She tried to set it in place with her hands to get a better idea of how she'd look on the evening but it wouldn't lie down. It was only just after it was washed and brushed that she was able to let it fall softly round her ears.

Out in the wind a minute, and she looked terrible. She'd tried everything. Perms—her hairdressers always said to her, "Your hair needs a little movement, madam," but they merely frizzed it. She stood there and thought Harry would like the silkiness of the dress if he touched it or if he placed his arm round her waist —Carmichael felt her colour mounting at the idea—but of course he wouldn't.

She shook herself almost angrily, pulled the dress over her head, draped it across the chair, and put on her jumper and skirt. She tied her head scarf on and went out into the shop, carrying the dress, wrote a cheque, and left the shop with a carrier in which the dress was neatly folded in tissue paper. She felt she had chosen well. For the moment, at least, she thought that; the doubts would follow, she knew. Doubts followed Carmichael like gnats on a sunny day.

The next thing she had to think of was the perfume. Chanel, that was what Miss Johnson had said. She winced a little at the thought of the price, but no, she would not be put off. Harry, if she passed him and a slight waft of lovely perfume followed her —surely it would make him feel that she was attractive. She paid what she considered was a colossal amount of money and came away with the tiniest of bottles. She loved the smell. She would like to use it for ever; she would be known by her perfume. Her purchases finished, she made her way back to her flat.

There were more arrangements to be made of course; she realized that as she put down her purchases. She must ring the hairdresser and get an appointment as late as possible on the Saturday. She hoped it wouldn't rain, that she wouldn't have to put a head scarf on. She thought of her plastic rain hat and then thought, Emily wouldn't be seen dead in a plastic rain hat.

Carmichael hung the dress on a hanger and hooked it on the front of her wardrobe. She was pleased to notice she was still satisfied with it. Then, cautiously, she took the small bottle of perfume, undid the seal, took out the frosted stopper, placed her finger over the top of the bottle, tipped it up, and then carefully put the stopper back. She smelled the tip of her finger, then rubbed it gently behind one ear and then the other. The perfume was really lovely, electrifying.

Makeup. She always used a pale lipstick—she thought it better with her sallow skin. She never asked or had instruction in a shop like some people did. She was too shy. Still, this Saturday she was going to make a special effort. She wondered what Emily would wear? She was imposing and good-looking. There was something vixenish about her face—men sometimes liked that. Still, never mind that. This evening with him, even with Emily sitting beside him at a table in a hotel, was going to be as perfect as she could make it. But she mustn't anticipate too much. She would just cling to the fact that she was going to be with Harry for the whole evening.

On Saturday morning she had a dress rehearsal. On the whole, she was pleased. She didn't get as far as putting on her makeup, although she'd even bought some pale green eye shadow. Carmichael hardly ate any lunch, partly because she was going to have dinner that night, but mostly because she was so nervous.

At the appointed time she was outside the Maitlands' house. She drew the car a little to one side so that she would not impede their car, which was already parked in front of the house. Once more she stood at that Tudor-type door—but under what different circumstances. She felt her heart beating one hundred and twenty pulses a minute. She knew, she was a nurse, she could tell.

"Calm down," she said to herself under her breath, then pulled the wrought iron bell. Almost before the clanging had ceased the door was opened, wide, by Harry.

"Is it . . . ?" he asked.

"Yes, it's Agnes." She got the words out with difficulty. Her mouth had suddenly gone completely dry and the palms of her hands were sticky. She clutched her evening bag in her hand and felt the moisture on its silver leather surface. She wasn't sure about evening bags, but it was all she had.

"Oh, great. You're in time for a drink before we go out." Harry walked purposefully across the hall and into the sitting room. "Emily's still getting ready. She takes a long time to get dressed. It's not that she leaves everything to the last minute—it's you ladies; you know how much longer you take to get ready than we do." He smiled at Carmichael, picking up the glasses and bringing them to where she was standing.

"I've given you sherry. Is that all right?" he asked.

Carmichael stood there in her green dress. She had dropped her camel-hair coat on the chair in the hall as she came through. Her hair just done, she held her head stiffly so as not to let stray pieces stick out as they did if she moved her head too much.

"That's lovely," she said. Oh, that blasted word! She wished she could lose it. But Harry did not appear to notice.

"That's an attractive perfume you're wearing. It smells like flowers, like a summer garden. I should think it matches you perfectly."

It was lightly and gallantly said, a remark that any man might make to any girl, any woman, but it seared Carmichael. Yes, it was exactly what she wanted the perfume to do, make him think that . . . She dismissed the tremor of apprehension that went through her. How could he ever know, really know, what she looked like? Only through something Emily might say and he'd hardly take much notice of that, and somehow Carmichael thought that Emily wasn't really interested enough to remark on her appearance. At that moment Emily swept down the stairs.

CHAPTER 11

To say that Emily swept down the stairs was the only way to describe her descent. Carmichael thought again what an imposing woman she was. She watched her with envy and with a sinking heart. Emily wore a long, black velvet evening dress, cut low; a gold chain and pendant, her only jewellery. The gold pendant rested on her milk white skin between her full breasts.

Her hair, dark and shining, was caught back in a large bun, low on her neck, from which little curls escaped. Carmichael felt herself shrinking, then tried to reassure herself—Harry can't see, he can't see, don't worry. He's seen Emily, yes, years ago, but probably if he saw her now he'd think she'd changed. Carmichael did notice, as Emily walked into the sitting room, a telltale thickening of the waist, the full chin that would soon become a double chin. But the skin on her neck and arms was still beautiful and unwrinkled, white, and fleshy. Carmichael sought for a word to describe her and thought "seductive."

"Hallo, you've arrived. Drink, Harry, please," Emily said. Harry went over to the bar cart and poured her a gin and tonic.

She sipped it, then said rather crossly, "It's warm. There's no ice in it. Didn't you get any ice out?"

"No, I didn't. I'll go and get some."

"Oh, it doesn't matter. You'll probably tip some water down your suit or something. No, I'll suffer it."

She drank the gin and tonic rapidly. "Well, shall we go?"

She seemed to take no notice at all of the fact that Carmichael's sherry glass was half full, as was Harry's.

"Okay," he said, amiably enough, and drained his glass. Carmichael did the same.

Emily Maitland looked at her critically. "There's no need to choke yourself, Miss Carmichael," she said, laughing, but the laugh was not friendly.

She turned round and made for the sitting-room door, picking up her mink jacket as she entered the hall. Harry followed her, and she handed the jacket to him. He held it up for her and she shrugged it on. Carmichael picked up her own camel coat.

Outside they got into the Maitlands' Rover, with Carmichael in the back. Emily Maitland opened the car door for herself and got in carefully, pulling her skirt in so that it didn't rub on the edge of the car door.

"Come on, Harry," she said impatiently.

Harry was just pushing the front door to see that the latch was firm and he came down the steps with the ease of long practice, put his hand out and felt the car in a way that made Carmichael's heart lurch with pity, found it, orientated himself to where he was in relation to the car, walked round the front, opened the door, and got in beside Emily.

"Are you all right, Agnes?" he said.

Carmichael answered him. "Yes, I'm fine, Harry, thank you. What a lovely car."

"Lovely car!" laughed Emily. "We want a new one. It isn't fast enough for me. I want a sports model. After all, I'm not that old yet that I can't have a sports car. I think I'll get one, Harry." It was obviously an argument of long standing.

"Very well, my dear, but we'd better keep this one, as I find it more comfortable."

Emily Maitland shrugged, but did not answer. They drove into the main road and away.

During the drive, which must have taken half an hour or more, Emily hardly spoke. Harry made one or two remarks to Agnes Carmichael, sitting mute in the back of the car, but she hardly took in what he said. She was assessing herself again and finding herself wanting.

I should have had a long dress. It would have been better if I'd worn my long skirt that I wore to the Ealing's. This is an afternoon frock, or a summer dress even; it's not suitable. She looked down at her silver sandals, which she'd had for ages, but the price of the dress had made her think twice about buying new shoes and, anyway, they matched her bag.

Carmichael longed to open her handbag, take out her compact and have a quick peep at her makeup. But she thought she'd better wait till they got to the inn, in the ladies' room, where they left their coats; even then she would be afraid to do anything in front of Emily Maitland. She had noticed Emily's lips as she had drunk the gin and tonic, the lovely outline—not like her own, which seemed to run in to the rest of the skin of her face, so that to make a clear line was almost impossible. By the time they arrived and drew in to the courtyard of the roadhouse, Carmichael had almost destroyed herself. Then, as she got out, she saw other people getting out of cars in dresses similar to her own, and this restored her confidence a little.

"Have you locked the door on your side, Harry?" Emily asked and he turned quickly.

"No, dear, sorry." He opened his door, put the catch down and slammed it to. Carmichael followed suit with the door at the back and Emily nodded approvingly.

"Thank you, Miss Carmichael. Harry always forgets to lock car doors. I think he likes to play the absentminded professor. He leaves windows open, remember?"

Harry didn't answer, but preceded them towards the door without assistance. He seemed to know his way, but when he got to the steps he misjudged them and stumbled slightly. Emily put out a hand and steadied him.

"For God's sake, let me go first, Harry. Don't show off just because Miss Carmichael is here."

Could she mean it or was it a joke? Carmichael couldn't tell, but to ease the tension she said suddenly and bravely, "Please don't call me Miss Carmichael. Do call me Agnes. It's not a name I like, but it's all I've got."

Emily Maitland hardly turned round but she acknowledged it with a nod and said, "Right. Agnes it is. No, I don't think much of the name myself, any more than I do Emily. I was called Emily after an aunt who left me quite a lot of money, so it paid off in the end. I suppose the same applies to you—you had a rich aunt, did you, or someone? That's the trouble with families, you get these ghastly names wished on you. Please call me Emily."

"No, it's nothing like that," said Carmichael and followed Emily, then Harry, into the inn.

The foyer was beautiful, softly lit and full of shining furniture. They walked through into the bar, Harry obviously at home here, as was Emily. Agnes Carmichael wished she could leave her coat somewhere. She wanted to be rid of it. She didn't want Harry to put his hand out near her and feel the camel hair; she wanted him to feel the silk of her dress.

"It's hot, isn't it?" she said, tentatively.

"I think it's chilly. If you want to leave your coat, do, but the bar is not all that warm, is it Harry?" Harry shook his head.

In the bar Harry ordered. They sat down at a table. He felt his way carefully, guided now and again by Emily's hand, the hand which Carmichael would have loved to have pushed out of the way and replaced it with her own.

The waiter put their drinks in front of them and the kind of small talk that Carmichael dreaded, began.

"We were talking about families and our names—what part of the world do you come from, Agnes?"

"Well, I was born in Hampshire," Carmichael hesitated before the word.

"Hampshire—oh, what part? I know Hampshire quite well. I used to sail a lot when I was young, didn't I, Harry?"

"We both did. It was one of our things, wasn't it, darling."

"I rather feel I would like to sail again. We were rather pot hunters, weren't we?"

Harry nodded. "We were. We did quite well until I . . . . You could always go down to the island, to your sister's, and have a sailing holiday. You know that. You might race again if you wish."

"No, I'm too old. Time's gone past. I couldn't bear it, I think now. No, I'll stick to my painting. I may have been good at sailing, but I think I'm better at painting."

There was a silence and Carmichael remembered the young man's remark at the Ealing cocktail party. She felt she had to fill in the silence.

"Yes, I heard at the Ealings' cocktail party that you painted."

"Did you. Well, I just hope that someone said something complimentary. They don't usually. No one in our circle understands my paintings in the least, but I'm negotiating for a London exhibition—there I will be understood. I'm looking forward to it. Well, I'm being pressed to do it . . ."

Harry broke in gently. "I'm afraid I'm quite incapable of criticising Emily's paintings. I'd very much like to see them. They sound—interesting." Harry finished his drink.

"Interesting! That's what everybody says who doesn't understand what the hell they're all about. I mean the one I call 'The Jump'—if anyone can't see what it is without me putting the title on I despair. Jeremy got the message in a moment. So many people think of pictures today in terms of money. Not that I shan't be pleased to sell some at my London exhibition. I realize it is the appreciation of your work that inspires people to buy."

"Yes, I suppose so." Carmichael was completely out of her depth. Again she remembered the young man's remark and wondered how Emily had managed to get a London exhibition.

"Another drink before we go in?" asked Harry. Carmichael refused, but Emily rose to her feet.

"Yes, I want one. Harry, you're right. You'd better not have one. I'll just get one for myself, if you don't mind waiting." She went off to the bar—rudely, Carmichael thought.

Harry must have felt this too, for he said, "Emily's very impetuous. You mustn't mind if she takes you up sometimes rather quickly."

"Yes . . . no . . . I hadn't noticed," Carmichael said lamely and then went on. "I'm glad that she's going to exhibit her paintings in London. Is it at the Royal Academy?"

Harry laughed and put out his hand suddenly, in search of Carmichael's. It was just a means of communication. He clasped her hand, then let it go and laughed again.

"No, not the Royal Academy, Agnes. Probably a little shop in Bond Street her friend Jeremy has found. They may even be charging her to hang her paintings. But if she sells one or two, well, it will be a great encouragement for her and we all need that, don't we?"

How patient, loyal, and understanding he is, thought Carmichael. He doesn't mind that his wife . . . that her paintings probably aren't any good. She suddenly decided that while Emily was away at the bar, whatever happened, she was going to get rid of her coat.

"Is there somewhere, Harry, I can put my coat? I do find it rather warm in here."

"Well, of course, just over there I believe is the ladies' room. If you like to go in and leave it with the attendant . . ."

"May I? Will you excuse me?" Carmichael wondered if it was right for a woman to excuse herself to a man, but it was too late now; she'd done it.

"Of course. We'll wait for you. Anyway Emily's got to finish her drink. Then she'll probably want to powder her nose too." He grinned an almost boyish grin at Carmichael and she got up, walked across the room self-consciously and in to the ladies' room.

There was an attendant there. The mirrors were pink. It was very luxurious, and it flashed through Carmichael's mind immediately, What ought I to give her when I go? She didn't look at the woman's face as she handed her her coat in case she should see something discouraging in her eyes. She walked over to the brightly lit mirrors. Her lipstick was still more or less in place, but she thought she'd put on a tiny bit more. She wondered if the smell of her perfume was disappearing; she couldn't smell it. She had brought the bottle in her handbag and now she took it out and put a tiny dab behind each ear and put the bottle back in her handbag. The powder at the end of her nose was beginning to clog and go an orangey colour—she had found the bar hot in spite of what they had said, mainly because her pulse rate was up so much, she thought, grimly; but there was dinner to be got through—how much more would it clog? Suddenly, she wished she hadn't come. She touched the end of her nose, tentatively, with a puff from her compact. At that moment Emily came in.

"Oh, there you are, Miss Car—Agnes," she said. "I must wee."

She went into one of the lavatories and Carmichael wondered whether to stay and wait for her or go out and back to Harry's table. She decided to wait. Emily came out of the lavatory, went over and peered at herself in the mirror over the wash basin, the tap of which she turned on automatically, put her fingers under it, and then turned to the attendant.

"May I have a towel, please?" The attendant immediately handed her a small linen towel. "Oh, well, I can't do any more about my face," glancing once more into the mirror.

"It looks very nice," said Carmichael and meant it.

What effect this had on Emily she had no idea; Emily threw her an amused glance, opened her bag, gave the attendant something, and then walked out. Carmichael, following meekly, wondered whether she, too, should give the attendant something, decided yes, and fumbled to open her silver bag. Emily looked round.

"That's okay," she said, so Carmichael snapped the bag shut and they went back to the table where Harry was sitting.

The waiter came up and said, "Your table's ready, sir," and they all three went into the restaurant, Emily leading, followed by Carmichael, then Harry.

Carmichael could not let him walk alone, she just could not. Whether Emily always did or whether she was just showing off Carmichael was not sure, but she dropped a step back and put her hand on Harry's arm. It was the most daring thing she'd ever done. He responded instantly and patted her hand.

"Thanks," he said. "I don't want to bump into a table and send somebody's dinner flying. There's nothing like a floor covered with food to annoy people," and he laughed and his laugh sounded real. Agnes felt for the first time that evening that she had done absolutely the right thing.

Then her brief confidence was shattered again. As they sat down at the table Emily said, "Oh-h, someone's rather overpowering with the perfume." She looked round the room, but Carmichael felt sure she meant her and wished she hadn't put any more on. However, it was done now.

Harry quickly filled in the gap by saying, "I think it's a lovely perfume. I can't have too much of it. I believe it's Agnes'."

CHAPTER 12

Emily opened the large menus and proceeded to order the meal for all three of them, making suggestions adroitly, telling the waiter quietly that her husband needed restricted carbohydrates. It was all done with such expertise. Carmichael felt that Emily would know how much to tip when the dinner was ended; she would scrutinize the bill and would not be afraid of saying something if she thought it was too much.

"Send me the wine waiter," Emily said and again Carmichael envied her and wondered what she would say when she was asked what wine she would like to drink. How she prayed and prayed for confidence.

Dinner was enjoyable, the food delicious, and Carmichael tried to dismiss everything from her mind except the fact that she was sitting beside her beloved Harry. When the wine waiter arrived everything went perfectly. Emily had him read out one or two of the names to Harry, who suggested which wine would go with the various courses, so Carmichael was spared any embarrassment, for which she thanked him silently with all her heart.

The conversation during dinner was carried on mostly between Harry and herself. Emily drank more wine than they and Carmichael thought briefly of the fact that she was driving them home, but then decided that obviously Emily was used to taking plenty of wine. At first it seemed to have no effect on her at all. Indeed, her look of enduring boredom remained unaltered throughout the meal until the sweet, when disaster happened.

"I'll have to pass this one. I'll have a little cheese," Harry said to the girl wheeling the sweet trolley, which was loaded with beautiful gateaux, caramel custard, fresh fruit salad, and an assortment of fruits and cream.

"Yes, sir, I'll get the waiter to bring the cheese board."

She wheeled the trolley between Emily and Agnes Carmi-chael. Emily chose a slice of coffee gateau. Carmichael, less ner-vous now, chose a gateau also, but one garnished with black cherries. She had never tasted black cherries and her mouth watered as she looked at them. The waitress cut a generous wedge and was about to hand it to Carmichael when the cheese waiter arrived at Harry's side. Carmichael looked at him and realized that Harry did not know the waiter was there, so she moved her hand to touch Harry's, to tell him. As she did so she knocked the plate of gateau out of the waitress' hand. There was a silence. Emily looked at Carmichael, looked at the floor, then at the waitress.

"Oh, I'm so sorry, I'm so terribly sorry." Carmichael looked at the mess the creamy gateau had made on the carpet by their table. The plate had rolled a little further and fallen unbroken with its creamy side down.

"Never mind. They'll soon clear it up and Harry won't mind paying for another slice."

Emily smiled benignly at the waitress who cut another slice of the gateau and put it in front of Agnes Carmichael with a determined thud. She wheeled the trolly away. A boy appeared a few minutes later wearing white trousers and a slightly grubby apron, summoned from the kitchen no doubt. He man-aged to clear up pretty speedily, Carmichael thought. He was about to get to his feet when Emily opened her bag, withdrew a folded pound note, holding it between the forefinger and second finger of her hand, and proffered it to the boy. From looking morose his face expanded in a smile.

"Thank you, madam," he said, and wiping his right hand on the side of his trousers, still kneeling on the floor, he took the pound and slipped it into the top pocket of his white shirt be-neath the bib of his apron. He got up and Emily nodded to him.

"You've done that very nicely. There's not a mark left."

"Not at all, madam, not at all. Glad to be able to help," the boy smirked at Emily.

Why, oh why, thought Carmichael, didn't I think to do that?

"I should have done that, I should have . . ."

"Please, don't let's make any more fuss about it, it's over and done with, don't think about it." Emily turned to her own plate.

"What's happened? What was it?" Harry had asked the cheese waiter to put a slice of cheddar on his plate and had waved away the biscuits and butter. "What happened?" he asked mildly but determinedly.

"Oh, just a little accident, that's all. Nothing much. Don't worry." Emily spoke in a terse, dismissive manner.

"Well, I'd like to know. It's a bit difficult you know when you can't see, Emily." Again his voice was mild, but there was an edge to it.

"It was me," said Carmichael, "it was all my fault. I knocked the plate of gateau out of the waitress' hand and it went all over the floor. A boy came and cleaned it up and—"

"Oh, please," said Emily wearily, and Carmichael realized she was making too much of it all, that people like them would just pay and dismiss it. But she had to explain, she had to.

Carmichael could see that Harry sensed the anguish in her voice. He put out his hand, found her arm, and patted the silk sleeve of her dress reassuringly.

"Oh, is that all? Don't worry about that. I do things like that all the time. I'm sure Emily worries about our carpet at home, don't you, Emily?" Emily did not reply. "Have you got some more—have you got what you want?" he asked Carmichael and she replied that she had.

She could hardly eat the gateau; the cherries tasted like ashes in her mouth. She managed to get it down because now and again Emily looked at her, assessing whether she had got over the incident, and Carmichael felt she must make no more fuss.

"Liqueurs for you too?" Harry asked. "I can't have them, I'm afraid. What would you like?"

The only liqueur that Carmichael knew was crème de menthe, so she said that hesitatingly and watched Emily's face. Did her mouth curl a little with a contemptuous smile? Carmichael couldn't be sure.

Emily turned and summoned a waiter and said, "One crème de menthe and one kümmel. That is all."

The waiter was about to leave when suddenly Harry said, "I'll have a brandy, I think."

"Is that wise?" said Emily. Her voice sounded uninterested but questioning. "You've had a little more than your carbohydrate ration, you know. It might be wiser not to have the brandy."

"But I'd like it, Emily. I feel a bit tired. I think it's all right."

"Very well, you know best," she turned to the waiter again. "And a brandy."

The man disappeared but soon returned with the small glasses, one green, one colorless like water, and a brandy. Carmichael smelled the faint smell of aniseed and wondered what kümmel tasted like. She would find out. She would buy a miniature of all the different liqueurs and taste them. She'd seen the little bottles in wine shops. Why hadn't she done it before? She should have educated herself about these things. The waiter put down the balloon glass with brandy in it in front of Harry. Carmichael tasted her pepperminty liqueur. The drink and the coffee soothed her jangled nerves a little. She knew that when she got home and assessed the evening then all the trouble would start, but for the moment she tried to put it away from her.

Back in the Rover they drove almost in silence to the Maitlands' house and into the drive.

Harry turned and said to Carmichael, "You'll come in for a nightcap, will you?"

Emily was silent. She didn't turn round or second the invitation.

Carmichael shook her head. "No, I don't think I'd better drink any more. I've got to drive, you know." She sounded arch and immediately criticized herself for that.

"Very well, then."

It was Emily who spoke. She got out of the car and came round and opened the door for Harry. He got out and in turn opened the back door for Carmichael and the three of them stood there for a moment by the car. The street lamp lighted up Emily's tall figure and her beautiful fur, her hair still immaculate and smooth. She carried her head a little high, her chin pointing slightly upward. Carmichael noted it. She would copy it; she would learn to walk and stand like that.

"Thank you both for a lovely evening and a beautiful dinner. I was so sorry to have—" She shouldn't have said that and she hastily amended it. "It was such a nice inn, really lovely. It was so kind of you both."

"Glad you liked it. It's not a bad place. Come along, Harry. You go in and I'll put the car away."

Harry held out his hand to Carmichael to say good-night, then felt his way round the car and unerringly towards his front steps. Carmichael watched him get his key out and put it in the lock.

Emily spoke again. "Excuse me, Agnes, but until you go, I can't get my car in the garage."

It was a dismissal and one which Carmichael felt she deserved. She had been standing there just watching Harry. She turned quickly.

"Oh, of course, I'm so sorry, I'll get on."

Emily walked round and got into the driver's seat and Carmichael walked towards her own Mini. She got in and drove carefully out of the gate. To hit one of their gate posts would indeed have been the end, she thought, her miserable mood coming back. As she drove through the gate, she heard Emily hoot behind her and wondered if she had touched the hooter by mistake. Then she realized that Emily was signalling to her, Carmichael, that she had not put her lights on. She switched them on hastily. Another mark against me, I suppose, she thought.

As she drove along the dark road, the car behind her suddenly illuminated the interior of the Mini. A quick glance into her mirror showed the disastrous effect of the evening on her hair. The final blow, she thought. She didn't know whether it had mattered or not—she felt curiously bewildered. She knew that her thoughts had not yet started turning evenly to take in the whole picture of her latest meeting with the man she was beginning to love more than her own life. Determinedly, she dismissed everything from her mind except driving the car. She would not think until she got back to the flat. She would feed Tibbles, get ready for bed. Then she would allow herself to think.

CHAPTER 13

On Monday morning Carmichael arrived at work white and tired. She had done exactly what she had determined in the car on her way home on the Saturday evening. She had thought out the whole evening when she got home. Tibbles had greeted her with great affection as usual. She had fed her. Then, keeping her mind determinedly blank, she had undressed, washed, got into her nightdress, filled a hot-water bottle, made herself a hot drink, and got into bed. The hot drink had cooled beside her as her thoughts traced back to when she had arrived at the Maitlands' house, the car ride, the dinner, the car ride back. What she had said, what they had said, and what she had done—what she had lost and what she had gained. The latter seemed almost imperceptible. She couldn't get the evening out of her mind and this had resulted in a second sleepless night on Sunday.

When she arrived in her office Johnson greeted her with: "What do you think! They've got some kind of bug on Men's Surgical. Three of them have got sore throats. They're having to have swabs taken; may have to cancel the ops. What a to-do! Surgeons moaning, pathologists carrying on about the extra work, I dunno. Nurses can take sudden crises, but doctors—it always seems to knock them to pieces. I must go. I may have to rearrange staff. One thing, the operating theatre is your department—I don't know what they're doing up there." She went out of the door, banging it behind her as usual.

Carmichael's mind would hardly take in what Johnson had said. Throats . . . Oh Lord. Haemolytic strep? Something like that. Well, she'd better go up to theatre; she'd better go and see what was happening. She hurried out of her office and up the stairs to the operating theatres. The OPERATION IN PROGRESS

light was out. She pushed open the door and peered in. All was
quiet. Two nurses were leaning against the theatre table talking.

"Where's Sister?" Carmichael's voice cut through their conversation and they hastily straightened up at the sight of her.

"She's having coffee in the doctors' room with . . ."

Carmichael didn't wait for them to finish. She pushed open
the swing doors and went into the surgeons' changing room.
Sister was sitting in her theatre garb, her legs crossed, showing
half way up her thigh, Carmichael thought with disgust and
annoyance. With her and beside her sat Mr. O'Connor, he had
not changed into theatre garb and did not rise when Carmichael
came into the room.

"A right balls-up," he said. "I don't know whether we're operating or not. Something on the Men's Ward, I dunno. Throats?
We're not told anything; we're the last people to know. Well, I'm
not changing, Miss Carmichael, not until I'm sure we're operating."

"I don't think we are," said Carmichael coldly, "so no doubt
you will be able to go down and do a ward round."

"How do you know I haven't got a sore throat?" said O'Connor rudely. It was obvious he couldn't stand Carmichael.

The Theatre Sister, who had risen hastily to her feet and put
her coffee cup down, said, "We are honestly waiting to be told.
We've just heard the rumour that the list is cancelled. Luckily
it's not a very long one, because Mr. Franton is away so it was
only Mr. O'Connor's list."

"Only Mr. O'Connor's list. Oh ta," said the Registrar, contin-
uing to sip his coffee.

"I'll go and see what's happening and let you know," said
Carmichael. "Then, if the theatre is not going to be used today,
we can put the nurses elsewhere. That is, if the infection war-
rants it." She swept out of the door, leaving, she knew, two
disgruntled people behind her. But that was not her worry.

Having found out that indeed it was true and that some of the
nurses were having throat swabs and that operations would be
temporarily discontinued, she went back to her office and
phoned the Theatre Sister, well satisfied with the ripples of dis-
content she had managed to start in various parts of the hospital.

It was nice to have authority somewhere, and the disaster of Saturday night receded a little. After all, here she was someone, and she was determined that she would learn, too, how to be as good outside the hospital as she was in it. She'd be able to cope with little things like liqueurs. She'd learn.

It was in this more ebullient mood, after she had returned to her office and told Johnson the news which had sent her scurrying off again, that she picked up the phone. She was determined to thank Harry for the dinner. She was about to ask the telephonist in the front hall for the Maitlands' home number when she decided against it. She made up her mind to ring the University and speak to Harry direct. Why not? She looked at her watch. He would probably only just have arrived there and in that case she wouldn't be interrupting him in anything. And even if she did, she was a friend. She must learn to be more like Emily. She asked the telephonist in the front hall to look up the number of the University and got a rather testy reply.

"I will when I have time, Miss Carmichael. I'm a bit pushed at the moment. You know what the early morning is for enquiries."

Carmichael put the phone down. It was true it was a bad time to ask for an outside number, but she didn't care.

Ten minutes later the phone rang and the telephonist gave her the number, asking at the same time, "Shall I get it for you, Miss Carmichael?"

Carmichael said "Yes" firmly.

"I'll ring you back then."

Carmichael put the phone down again. This time five minutes passed before it rang again and a voice said, "Professor Maitland's office. Can I help you?"

Carmichael breathed a sigh half of relief and half of fright. Had she done the wrong thing in ringing him there? The voice sounded pleasant enough.

"I only wanted to speak to Professor Maitland for a moment. Perhaps he's lecturing?"

"No. Professor Maitland is not at the University today. Are you a friend of his?"

"Yes, yes, indeed I am. Is he lecturing somewhere else, or is it not possible to . . ." Carmichael felt again hopelessly inadequate.

"Professor Maitland is unwell. He's at home today."

Carmichael's heart seemed almost to stop.

"Unwell. Oh, I'm so sorry. I hope it's nothing serious. I was with him on Saturday evening. I hope—"

The voice at the other end of the phone became slightly more detached. "I really don't know. Mrs. Maitland rang in this morning to say that the Professor was unwell and wouldn't be in. Perhaps if you rang his home you might be able to learn more."

"Thank you, I'll do that."

Carmichael put the phone down and found that her hand was wet with sweat. Ill? What was the matter with him? Was it his heart? This heart condition that she could find nothing about in his notes? Was it his diabetes? Had he gone into a coma? Had Emily been right at the dinner? Had he eaten too much carbohydrate? Oh God, she must ring up. He probably wouldn't want her to, wouldn't want her even to know that he was ill, but . . .

She picked up the phone again and asked for his number.

The switchboard girl said, "All right. When I can," but Carmichael hardly heard her. When the phone rang, her hand trembled as she picked it up.

"Yes, who is it? Yes, she's in, yes. I'll get her." It was an unknown voice, probably Carmichael guessed, the cleaning woman. There was a pause and a clicking noise, perhaps made by her own switchboard—she couldn't tell. She waited a long time. After what seemed minutes, Emily Maitland came on the phone.

"Who is it?" Her tone was crisp, but then it usually was.

"It's Miss Carmichael. Agnes. I rang Harry at the University to thank him for the lovely evening, but they said he was unwell and suggested that I ring his home. So I thought . . ." As usual with Emily, Carmichael felt herself going to pieces.

"Oh, I see. You rang the University first. Well, no, Harry's not there . . . He's having a day off. A little trouble with his diabetes; nothing to worry about."

"May I come and see him?" Carmichael dared to say this; the surprise in the voice at the other end was evident.

"H-m, yes, I suppose so. You are a nurse. You know that he must be kept quiet. Perhaps you'd like to ring again in a day or so, though he may be back at the University by then. I really don't know. It all depends on the doctor, and you know how cagey they are—you work with them." The phone was put down.

Carmichael put hers down and she felt ill herself. Her mind pictured terrible things happening, perhaps him dying before she ever saw him again.

She put her head in her hands for a moment. It was too much. She almost wished she'd never met Harry Maitland, that she was still just Nursing Officer Carmichael, with a nice flat and Tibbles . . . But then, to know him was the most wonderful thing that had happened in her life, so how could she really think that? She withdrew her hands from her face and pulled a sheet of paper towards her, looked at the typing on it in a daze, then shook herself, and determinedly began to read: "Instructions for" . . . for what? . . . "stomach wash out," she read, and gradually the words began to make sense.

CHAPTER 14

Several times in the next two days Carmichael picked up the phone ready to ask the front-hall telephonist for an outside number—and then put it down again. She was fearful that Harry would be back at the University and she would get an impatient Emily. She thought about Harry constantly, wondering how he was, and even played with the idea of calling one evening after work, at drinks time—people did that she was sure, but her courage failed her on both evenings. On the third morning she had almost made up her mind to phone when she got a surprise. As she was reaching out, full of determination, to ask for the Maitland number, her phone rang.

"Yes, Miss Carmichael here," she said in her usual brusque unemotional tone.

"There's a lady here to see you—a Mrs. Maitland. She would like to know if she could have a word with you and I said I didn't know whether you would want to come down here or have her come up to your office—I've put her in the front hall." The voice lowered a little. "She's a bit Private, know what I mean?"

"Yes." Carmichael thought quickly. "Will you get the receptionist to bring her up to the rest room on the Private floor and I'll go along and meet her there. Will that be all right?"

"Up to you. I'll tell Mrs. Long to conduct her up there—she looks as if she'll want a bit of conducting—ushering," said the telephonist sarcastically.

"Thank you, I'll meet her there." Carmichael put the phone down—she was trembling, trembling at the thought of meeting Emily Maitland.

She tried to pull herself together—tell herself that here she was someone on her own ground and Emily was the visitor—

but what could she want? Was he worse, was Harry worse? But surely, she wouldn't come and tell her? No. Carmichael couldn't imagine why Emily Maitland would come to see her and the only way to find out was to go to the rest room and meet her.

Walking round to the Private floor, she prayed the rest room would be empty. She hurried a little so as to be there before Emily Maitland. In this she was not successful. As she opened the door Emily Maitland was standing in the middle of the room.

She greeted Carmichael with the words "Ah, Agnes. May I smoke? Is there an ashtray anywhere?"

Carmichael looked round, saw one on the window ledge, and brought it over to the small table beside one of the green, plastic armchairs. Emily sat down.

"I hope you won't mind—my coming and asking you a favour, I mean. Do sit down Miss Carmichael. It makes me nervous when people stand up."

Carmichael hastily sat down on the edge of the chair. Even here, she thought, she can boss me around.

She stiffened her back a little and said in her most official voice, "What can I do for you, Emily?"

"Well, it's Harry," Emily went on, inhaling deeply on her cigarette and throwing the match towards the ashtray and missing. "He's not been too well since we went out to that dinner. It often upsets him, that sort of thing, but this time it's worse than usual. His diabetes has become unstabilized and he doesn't want to go into hospital. He's having to have two injections of insulin a day. His doctor is going away and the friend I could ask to come in, Margaret Tarrant, is coming with me to the exhibition. I'm determined to have her with me; I must have some support. It's rather an anxious time for me. I thought—" She stopped.

Carmichael's heart seemed to be dancing. Was she going to ask her to be with him, to stay, to look after him? She was.

"Normally, of course, I could get a nurse to come in and give the injections, but that means she'd only be there for a short time in the morning and in the evening. And when he's like this, I'm always a bit worried that he might go in to one of those awful comas—he had one insulin coma at home which frightened me to death."

Carmichael nodded. "Well, of course I'll be delighted to help you. Most certainly. When would you want me to come?"

"Well, I feel it's rather an imposition really, but if you could come on Saturday—sometime in the late morning? Mrs. Greenwood will be there until noon."

"Of course. Of course I will. And you want me to stay—"

"It's like this. My exhibition is on the Saturday—it's the only day we could get the gallery. Well, it's a special little show, you see—specially for me. And Jeremy he's tried so hard to get this. It's unusual to have a Saturday exhibition, but, well, until they know me, it's really all my pictures rate. You understand?"

Carmichael had never known Emily so voluble and she nodded.

"We have got a cousin who would come in and she has given the injections before, but Harry doesn't like her—she's rather overbearing—and he feels he would be much happier with you there."

Carmichael grabbed and treasured the word "happier" and wondered if he had really said that.

"I must go to London and I must stay the night. After all, we will have to bring the pictures back with us, and Jeremy . . ." Emily paused and her eyes met Carmichael's. Did the colour rise in Emily's cheeks? Carmichael wasn't sure. "Jeremy has taken such trouble about all this. After all, it is my big chance and I can't let him down—not possibly. I can't let Jeremy down. Will you?"

Carmichael felt that Emily loved using the word "Jeremy," loved repeating his name, rather like she did Harry's. Now she understood this feeling and she looked at her, bemused for a moment, before she answered her.

"Well, of course, of course. I'll come about twelve on Saturday, if you think that's all right, or before."

"No. As I said, Mrs. Greenwood is going to be there in the morning until twelve and she'll give him his lunch and I will have given him his injection at eight. It's just a question of someone being with him after Mrs. Greenwood has gone, and then, well, his urine will have to be tested before the evening injection. Is it too much to ask? You know how to vary the insulin and, well . . ." Emily tailed off. She was anxious, Carmichael could see. Carmichael, for once, was in the driving seat.

Emily went on. "I've written everything down for you." She snapped open her bag, took out a small notebook, and handed it to Carmichael. "The doctor filled that in for me. You can see the date." Carmichael leafed through the pages. "You have to put down what colour the stick is, you know, and vary the units of insulin accordingly."

"Of course." Carmichael managed to make the remark sound rather lofty. "I do hope you have a very successful exhibition and sell some of your paintings."

Emily lighted another cigarette and looked at Carmichael with slightly more interest.

"Thank you. That's nice of you. Margaret coming with me is a help, because—well, to be honest, it's rather an anxious-making time, you know, seeing your stuff hung up there. And I'm lucky even to get in on a Saturday. Walking among people and hearing their comments can be most unnerving and Margaret's a sympathetic person. I shall like to have her with me."

Carmichael nodded. She didn't know who the friend was, but she was obviously someone who understood Emily and perhaps even liked and approved of her paintings—understood them. Carmichael didn't care who it was. She and Emily could be out of the way while Carmichael was with Harry for just as long as they liked.

Emily rose, stubbing her cigarette out in the ashtray as she did so and brushing down the front of her smart black suit. She pulled on a pair of gloves, picked up her handbag, and walked toward the door. Carmichael followed her down to the front door of the hospital.

"They wouldn't let me bring the car in—well, I did bring it in, but they said I had to take it out again. It was reserved for Consultants, so I had to put it out in the road. Rather naughty, isn't it? I mean there should be a place for—"

"Yes, I know. It is difficult, but there's only just enough room in the courtyard for all the Consultants' cars, so of course—"

"Well, I suppose so. Your little Mini's there though. I saw it."

"Yes, well, I'm a Nursing Officer, you see."

Carmichael loved saying that, even if it did cause a slight twisted smile, a sarcastic look on Emily's face. She walked down the steps gracefully. Carmichael turned back into the hospital.

"A very Private type, eh?" The receptionist glanced at her with a grin. Carmichael nodded.

"Yes," she said. "I imagine she would be, if she got ill, and who knows, one day she may . . . I don't think she'd be a popular patient." This remark caused the receptionist's grin to fade a little. Carmichael's remarks always seemed to have a vague threat in them. She watched Carmichael walk up the stairs to her office.

"Your phone's been ringing," said Johnson as she walked in. "I answered it and it's a report from the pathologist, I think. Probably the haemolytic strep—operating theatre—you know. I told them to ring you back. They said they would." Carmichael could not draw her mind back could not react for a moment and Johnson went on, impatiently. "Wake up, dear. You know it may be that the theatre can go on operating—perhaps you'd better ring them. It was the pathologist who rang—you can ring the secretary if you like. He'll probably know." Carmichael shook herself.

"Oh yes, I will," she sat down at her desk but did not ring for a few moments.

She felt Johnson watching her. She decided that she wouldn't ring. She would go over to the Path. Lab. and see the pathologist herself and then up to the operating theatres. The need to walk about, to hide her delight, was so great that she felt movement was better than sitting phoning. She might even sound distracted on the phone, for she felt distracted.

In the Path. Lab. they told her that the nurses' swabs had been negative and that the operating could continue. She made her way up to the operating theatres; they knew, but listened to Carmichael. It was better to listen; Carmichael did not like to be interrupted when she was conveying a message. She was getting back into the swim of things, although the delight still lay at the back of her mind.

"You understand? Now what about this morning's list—how will you catch up?"

"Dunno," Sister said. "I'll have to leave it to Mr. O'Connor. Luckily, it was only minor things, as the Consultant's away. I guess we'll have to fit them in tomorrow, or the next day. The patients have been given breakfast now."

"The patients are in the beds, you know. They've been disappointed once," Carmichael said briskly and Sister nodded.

"Yeah. Oh, here he is." At that moment Mr. O'Connor walked in.

"All clear, I hear," he said, nodding at Carmichael and smiling at the Theatre Sister. "When can I have the theatre, then, for those four? They won't take all that long."

"We could do them this evening."

"Oh God. I was going out tonight, taking Jenny . . ."

Carmichael's raised eyebrows stopped him. "The patients are in, you know, Mr. O'Connor. They weren't sent home. I think it would be a good idea if you put them in as soon as possible. How about this evening, Sister? You were saying . . . ?"

"Well, it is clear. It might mean that if emergencies came in, they'd be later still." Theatre Sister walked into her office, followed by Carmichael and O'Connor, and flicked open the book on her desk. "Yes, the E.N.T. list isn't very long. You could be finished by four and have the theatre ready again by five." Carmichael looked enquiringly at Mr. O'Connor.

"Five. That's not so bad. I could be finished by seven," he said.

"I doubt it," said Sister, "You're not all that quick on varicose veins."

O'Connor nodded. "Well, counting the time it takes them to get the patients up from the ward and the anaesthetist being late, say, seven-thirty then. If I could do that, I could keep my date."

"I think the patients come first and are more important than your date, Mr. O'Connor," said Carmichael.

She did not wait for him to answer her, but pushed open the theatre doors and began to make her way down the stairs. The moment she was out of sight and sound of them, the weekend ahead came back to her. Joy flooded over her. She could have been much more terse with O'Connor and the Theatre Sister, but somehow she didn't want to be. When she entered her office again, there was a wide smile on her face and Johnson noticed it.

"Everything in the garden rosy?" she said and Carmichael looked at her, still bemused, and then snapped herself back to reality.

"Yes, everything in the garden is very rosy, thank you," she said and tried to wipe the smile off her face, but it still lingered slightly.

Johnson shrugged and under her breath said, "You look as if you're in love."

Carmichael heard her and to her astonishment her face turned scarlet.

"Don't be silly, Johnson," she said, but she said it, Johnson noted, without any conviction.

CHAPTER 15

The hours between dragged for Carmichael. She even went to bed early to make the time go by more quickly. She planned to get there about eleven, well before Mrs. Greenwood left, to find out what arrangements had been made as to Harry's food. Eleven would do.

What to take? Should she take the green dress to put on in the evening? They would be having dinner together, alone. Would they have it in the dining room? Or perhaps on a trolley or a tray in front of the fire? She had no idea—no idea how he lived when there were no guests. After all, she could hardly be thought of as a guest—she was there as a friend, looking after him, called in rather than the bossy cousin.

Well, Harry could relax while she was there. He could feel safe and needn't worry about anything that might happen to him. She thought it might be embarrassing asking for his specimen of urine, but he would know what to do so as not to embarrass her. Anyway, why should she think she would be embarrassed? She was after all, a nurse. She shied away from the thought. The testing of the urine, the giving of the injection, made her feel less like a friend and more like a nurse who had been asked to stay. She wouldn't think of that. She'd think more of the meal and of listening to music sitting beside him. She would try and make proper comments about it; not use the word "lovely." Really musical people—they just know what to say, know how to appreciate it.

She would be careful in her remarks. She would be guarded, not overenthusiastic; just listen quietly. She hoped he would put his hand out towards her and feel the silk of her dress—yes, she would change into that. She would take it with her, that and her night things. She supposed that Emily would put her in the spare room; that would be upstairs, away from Harry. Perhaps she'd just pretend to go upstairs and then sleep on the sofa in the sitting room in case he called or needed her. After all, insulin shock . . . she must look it up.

She went to the nurses' library and got out a medical book and read carefully through what she knew already. She just wanted to be doubly sure, just in case anything new had . . .

All this preparation made the time go by a tiny bit faster. Then, there was Tibbles. Tibbles couldn't be just left. She mustn't forget that Tibbles was her only companion before she had met Harry and the one in all the world that loved her most.

On Thursday evening she decided to make arrangements for Tibbles. She walked down the hall, leaving her own front door on the latch, and knocked. The door was opened by an elderly lady with white hair and a sweet, smiling face.

"Hallo, it isn't often you call on me, Miss Carmichael. What a pleasant surprise. Do come in."

"Thank you, but I'm afraid I've come to ask a favour."

"Well, if I can grant it, you know I certainly will. Is it Tibbles?" Mrs. Jenks' face had lighted up as she mentioned the cat's name. She had looked after Tibbles before, when Carmichael had stayed out till midnight with Jones' mother.

"Yes, it is Tibbles. I'm going away for the night, on Saturday. I shall be back again on Sunday, but I wondered . . . ? Tibbles won't understand. She hasn't been left before, not all night. I wouldn't like to think of her frightened; miaowing, crying—you know, she might—"

Mrs. Jenks broke in quickly. "She can stay here with me. She often visits me. She loves being in my flat. As you know, it's her second home. Of course I'll have her. I shall be delighted, I'll get her in on Saturday about four, if she's in your flat—"

"I'll give you the key of my flat, so that if she goes in there, you'll be able to fetch her out and bring her in here. And I'll bring her bed and blanket."

"That will be perfect. If she's got her own bed and her own blanket, she'll soon settle down. She'll be quite happy to sleep here. I'll have her in my bedroom. I love Tibbles, you know that."

"I'll be leaving on Saturday morning and I won't be back till midday or after on Sunday—I'm not sure. It's rather a long time, but I'll leave you the food and everything."

"Of course, my dear. If you want to take a week's holiday any time, you know Tibbles will be welcome."

Carmichael nodded. It was true; Tibbles was devoted to Mrs. Jenks. At first Carmichael had been a little jealous, but common sense had prevailed and she realized that the cat being alone all day was bound to give affection to someone who made a fuss of her, as Mrs. Jenks did. Now it was proving a boon. She thanked her neighbour, finished the arrangements about the milk and the cat's food.

"You needn't worry with all that, dear, I can get her milk—cream, if she wants it." Mrs. Jenks laughed and Carmichael smiled.

"Now, don't go and spoil her," she said and Mrs. Jenks shook her head.

Carmichael left feeling much happier. She didn't want to have to worry about Tibbles when she was with Harry, and after all, supposing Emily didn't come back on Sunday? It might be two nights. She knew Mrs. Jenks wouldn't mind, that she'd be delighted to have the cat, so that was all right.

Next evening Carmichael packed a small suitcase—just a nightdress, dressing gown, slippers, toilet necessities, and the green dress. She smiled in anticipation as she did this. She hadn't thought there would be a chance to wear it again so soon.

The small case packed, she went to bed and lay for a long time on her back, her hands under her head, staring into the darkness. After a while Tibbles jumped on to the end of the bed, curled herself up, and lay there purring.

Carmichael couldn't sleep, but she didn't mind. Every time she thought of tomorrow her heart lifted and a thrill went through her. She longed for the time when she could walk out of the flat, get into the Mini, and go towards that beloved man. At last, when it was nearly dawn, she fell asleep only to dream of him.

"Oh, you're here." This obvious statement was made by Mrs. Greenwood as she opened the door to Carmichael. Carmichael had come early. She couldn't keep away any longer once she thought that Emily Maitland must have departed for London. She looked self-consciously at her watch as she stood on the doorstep.

"Oh, I didn't realize that it was so early. Does it matter?"

Mrs. Greenwood stood back and let her in. "No, of course not, I shall be going at twelve anyway. I've nearly finished. I'm just getting lunch ready."

She led Carmichael through into the sitting room, then noticed the suitcase.

"Oh, of course. Mrs. Maitland said you were staying the night. You'd better come up and see your room, then."

They walked across the hall, Carmichael glancing at Harry's closed bedroom door. Up the stairs Mrs. Greenwood ushered her into a pleasant bedroom, not large, but beautifully appointed. The window was slightly open and the curtains moved softly in the breeze. They were rich, long curtains. Carmichael looked round the room. Everything in it spoke of wealth and taste.

"Well, I'll leave you to unpack. Then come downstairs and I'll make you a cup of coffee, if you like." Mrs. Greenwood left without waiting for Carmichael's reply. She had not spoken of Harry.

Carmichael hung up the green dress in the empty wardrobe and took out her toilet things and put them on the dressing table. Then she went downstairs and walked rather aimlessly across the hall and into the sitting room.

Except for a slight noise of crockery in the kitchen, the house was entirely silent. She sat down on the settee, opened a magazine on the coffee table, and thumbed through it. *Harpers.* She looked at the long-legged girls in their beautiful clothes, at their tousled hair piled high above their petulant faces, the full sensuous lips. The pictures made her feel ugly. She closed the magazine as Mrs. Greenwood walked in bearing a cup of coffee.

"It's a bit late for it, but I don't know when the Professor will be back. When you've finished, would you like to see . . . ?

Have your coffee. Then come through to the kitchen and I'll
show you where things are." Carmichael nodded and half rose.
"No, have your coffee first, or it'll get cold."

Mrs. Greenwood turned her back and walked out of the door
and Carmichael felt that she had summed her up, taken her in
for what she was—just nobody. She kept Mrs. Greenwood waiting for about ten minutes while she finished the coffee, then
took the coffee cup and saucer in her hand and made towards
the sound of running water and rattling crockery, which told
her where the kitchen was. She went through the swing door
and there was Mrs. Greenwood just putting the finishing
touches to a bowl of salad.

"There's the tomatoes. I've cut them up. Look, in that dish.
And there's the cucumber how he likes it. And I've tossed the
lettuce—he likes the French dressing I make. I hope you do
too." She went to the refrigerator door and opened it. "There's
the salmon. He likes salmon and he can have that. Then tonight
there's—"

"Is the Professor . . . ? Where is he?" Carmichael suddenly
couldn't wait any longer to know.

"He's at the University. A friend drove him there. He's coming back to lunch and he's not going back again—at least, that's
what he said. You're going to give him his injection tonight and
see he's all right, aren't you?"

Carmichael nodded and her eyes strayed round the kitchen,
but Mrs. Greenwood brought her back sharply.

"Look, you'd better look, nurse," she said.

Carmichael was furious. "I'm not a nurse. I'm a Nursing Officer at the hospital and I've come here just as a friend to help."
When she looked back at Mrs. Greenwood the woman's face was
bland enough.

"Oh, yes, of course. There's avocado pear there, with shrimps.
I did that this morning; in that little dish, see? That's the dressing for it. He can't have mayonnaise, but there's mayonnaise in
that little jug for you. Then, you turn the oven on about six
o'clock at four hundred. Or three-fifty, if you like—according to
when you want to eat. He likes to eat about eight. There's a
casserole in there. No potatoes, of course, for him. But he can

have one small one, so I've peeled it. If you like to boil it, there's one each for you."

Carmichael nodded, dumbly.

"I'm used to it, you see, used to getting things for him. Mrs. Maitland cooks a bit. She's very good. She does more complicated things. I do the plain. Get the vegetables ready, you know. When they have a dinner party, they have a special cook in and he brings a washer-up. He's quite well known. That's how they do it, you see. Well, they've got plenty of money, so why shouldn't they, I say."

Mrs. Greenwood sounded proud of the Maitlands. She turned to the kitchen door, took down a coat and shrugged it on, took a head scarf out of the pocket and tied it firmly under her chin, and picked up her basket.

"Okay. Have I told you everything I should? He'll be in for lunch as I said." She looked up at the electric clock in the kitchen and added, "In a bit." She looked at Carmichael's closed face curiously.

Carmichael was wondering, did Mrs. Greenwood know how the relationship had started? That she had met him at the hospital, rescued him from the burglar? She wondered just how much Emily Maitland talked to Mrs. Greenwood. Anything remotely flattering she could have said about her would have helped, but she knew she mustn't ask Mrs. Greenwood what the master or mistress of the house said.

As if her thoughts were transferred, Mrs. Greenwood said suddenly, "You're the one who rescued him from the burglar, aren't you? It was a good job you were going by. He wouldn't have seen him, would he? Mrs. Maitland told me about it. She was furious that he didn't shut the window. He does forget things, but then he's a Professor, isn't he? She doesn't care much. She has boyfriends you know. The new one, Jeremy—I expect you've heard about him. She's always got one and she always talks about them."

Carmichael's face reddened. She wanted to stop Mrs. Greenwood, as she knew a person of breeding would, but she couldn't. She was too anxious to know.

"Boyfriends?"

"That's right. She knows I know. She doesn't care. It's my belief he knows as much about them as I do. Oh, she goes off every now and again. Says she's going here or there. Hasn't been able to lately—that's why she's fed up, 'cause she can't get away. Bridge—oh, she plays bridge, but it's not bridge all the time. She can't pull the wool over my eyes. I've taken one or two phone calls."

She giggled, pulled the knot of the head scarf tighter under her chin, and went on. "Can't blame her, really. I mean, with him being blind and a diabetic and everything. Oh, he's nice enough, but she's a bit of a goer, you know. Not bad looking. She's going off a bit now. Overblown, that's what my husband calls her. He comes here sometimes to garden. Good word that —overblown—isn't it? Know what it means?"

Carmichael nodded her head dumbly. It was no good—she was on a level with Mrs. Greenwood now and there was nothing she could do about it. But she had learned something that made her feel better. Mrs. Greenwood made for the front door.

"What about his heart?" Carmichael suddenly blurted it out and Mrs. Greenwood turned, her hand on the handle of the front door.

"His . . . his what? Oh-h, his heart. Oh that. There's nothing the matter with his heart. But I happen to know"—she came very close to Carmichael—"I happen to know the Professor came home unexpectedly one day, and I put two and two together. He found them in bed, upstairs, Emily and the boy-friend. From that day, he never went up there again. He moved into the guest annexe down here. Nice in there, it is; bathroom and everything. Anyway, they don't sleep together now, so that's that. Emily tells people his heart's dicky and he doesn't want to do the stairs. Ah well, you know, they do funny things, don't they, people like them? Still, as I say, why not have a bit of fun if you can. Wish I could sometimes."

Mrs. Greenwood turned again to the door and Carmichael stood, speechless, in the middle of the hall. So that was why he slept downstairs. A warmth flooded through her. He couldn't . . . he didn't like Emily . . . How could he love a woman—if what Mrs. Greenwood said was true—that he had found in bed with a boyfriend? How it must have hurt him. She shook her head and Mrs. Greenwood watched her.

"What's the matter?" And as Carmichael didn't answer her, she went on opening the front door. "Hope I've told you everything I should. I think I have. You did find out where the loo was and all that? I put towels out for you; they're the pink ones. Yes, I think that's everything."

"Yes, thank you, I'm sure you have."

Carmichael tried to use the manner that she thought Mrs. Maitland would use toward Mrs. Greenwood, though at the back of her mind she felt it was too late. She'd been too matey. But then, she had learned . . . She closed the front door softly behind Mrs. Greenwood, then went back to the side window and watched her down the drive and out of the gate.

"Thank God, she's gone," she said to herself. "Now, when he comes back, I'll be alone with him."

She wandered back into the kitchen and looked at the arrangements for lunch; that was easy. She looked at the clock—twenty to one. She wondered whether she should take the salad into the dining room? Yes, she would. She took that and the salmon and put them on the table. She realized that she would have to serve the salmon. Mrs. Greenwood had laid the table. Wine glasses— did they have wine at lunch? Carmichael had seen a bottle of wine in the refrigerator. Should she get a jug of water and put it on the table? That might be the wrong thing. No, she would wait; see what he said when he came in. She would ask him if he had wine with his luncheon.

She wandered about the house, opened his bedroom door, and peeped in. It was a real man's bedroom, she thought. She withdrew hastily as she heard a key turn in the lock of the front door. She closed the door of his bedroom, gently, walked back into the middle of the hall and stood there, waiting.

CHAPTER 16

"Ah, Miss Carmichael. Agnes. You're here. I know by your perfume."

Carmichael was pleased. Harry Maitland closed the front door behind him and came towards her.

"This is very good of you to come, it really is. I might make a mess of things. It's very difficult when the insulin has to be changed in the evening, according to the test, you know. Then supposing I left a window open and you weren't there opposite, guarding me?"

Carmichael took the remark as it was meant, although it did not entirely please her.

"I'm very pleased to be able to help," she said.

"Shall we have a dry sherry before lunch? Would you like that?" he said.

Carmichael said, "Yes," with enthusiasm. She didn't particularly want the sherry. She just wanted to be with him. They went into the sitting room and the same routine followed as before.

"I always give you sherry," he said. "Perhaps you'd like something else? A gin and tonic or—" Carmichael hastily took the sherry from his hand.

"No, no, sherry's lovely," she said and then regretted the word "lovely" as usual.

"Do you smoke?" he asked.

"No, I don't. I don't indeed," said Carmichael a reproving note in her voice and, to her horror, saw him get out a cigarette case. Gold.

He opened it, took out a cigarette and tapped it on the case, put the case away, took out a small gold lighter, and lit the cigarette.

"Well, I'm ashamed to say I do. I haven't many vices now, but that's one of them."

He laughed. He looked, Carmichael thought, extremely well. She'd half hoped that he would look pale and wan and as if he needed her very badly.

"How are you feeling? Was it the—?"

"Oh, the old sugar again. A nuisance. I was nicely stabilized, I thought but . . . Emily persists it was that dinner we went to, but that's quite wrong. I haven't felt quite right for some days. I had a feeling—I'm experienced now—I know when my sugar's going up. It's a nuisance that I can't test my own urine. Then I could see how things were going. But Emily does it for me very kindly, or the doctor. And when I asked her to, well, there was a lot of sugar. The doctor came and took a blood test and said I ought to go into hospital to be restabilized, but I wouldn't. I hate it in there—not that they're not awfully kind, but I feel so tied down."

"I can understand that, but you must be careful."

"I will, and you're here to see that I'm careful. For the next day anyway."

"I hope Emily's exhibition will be a success."

"So do I. Her friend's going with her for moral support and I feel she'll need it. Critics can be devastating."

"Perhaps they'll like them. The people who come to the exhibition, I mean."

Harry drew heavily on his cigarette. "I hope so for Emily's sake, but Margaret will smooth her down if she gets upset."

"Margaret?"

"Yes, she's a great friend of ours. She lives just up the road. She lost her husband some time ago. She's here quite a lot. A very nice person, I'm glad she's with Emily."

Well, I'm with you today, thought Carmichael as she sipped her sherry. It was enough to sit silently and watch him smoking his cigarette, feeling along the coffee table for the ashtray. She watched him stub out the cigarette.

"I won't smoke another, or I shall feel your disapproval." He laughed.

"No, no."

"Shall we go through? Is lunch ready?"

"Yes, everything is ready. Mrs. Greenwood was very good and she has told me where everything is. It's in the dining room . . . I see she's put wine glasses out. Do you want some wine?"

"Do you? You're the guest," said Harry, smiling at her. "I won't have any, thank you, but please, please have a glass yourself. I'm sure there is a bottle in the—"

"No, thank you. I don't like to drink at lunch time. It makes me sleepy if I have wine." Carmichael had never had wine at lunch in her life, but she tried to lie glibly.

"Well, you won't have much to do this afternoon. I should go for a drive, if I were you. I've got to go back to the University, but I'll be back about five."

On an impulse Carmichael said, "Do you remember, once long ago, when you were walking by the Catholic church, I came out and bumped into you?"

She felt as though a great deal depended on what his reply would be and yet how could she expect him to remember? He didn't.

"No, I can't say I do remember," he said, looking at her curiously as they both stood in the doorway of the sitting room.

"No, I didn't think you would. Why should you? That was the first time we met and I remembered you when I saw you sitting in the Eye department."

"Oh, I see. How strange . . . and how clever of you." Harry turned and went toward the dining room.

That meeting meant nothing to him, Carmichael realized, but then why should it? It was to her that it meant everything. She wondered for a second, as she followed him into the dining room, whether that meeting had been for good or for ill. If she had not bumped into him and he had not held her for a second or two, she wouldn't have recognized him when he was waiting to see Mr. Ealing. No, it was fate, she supposed, but she wished that he had remembered.

Lunch was an easy meal, in spite of the fact that Carmichael's heart was racing as she sat down.

"It's salmon and salad. Shall I . . . ?"

"Please do. Not too much. Well, you know, don't you? Put some salad on the plate, too, if you will."

Carmichael began to put the food onto the plate and the very act seemed to her wonderful—wonderful that she was able to do something for him that he had asked her to do and would not in any way violate his independence.

It was not a talkative meal. She thought that Harry was preoccupied, probably with a lecture he was about to give and the papers he was to collect for it this afternoon, so she kept the silence and did not attempt to break it.

When he had gone, a light seemed to have gone out in the house and Carmichael walked about aimlessly. She went into his bedroom, looked round; went into the small bathroom, opened the cabinet door to see if she could see the insulin. Yes, there it was, and the syringes, all neatly laid out. She closed the bathroom cabinet, came out, shutting his bedroom door softly behind her as if there was someone in the house to hear. She went upstairs into Emily's bedroom, looked at the twin beds, and tried to visualize the scene that Mrs. Greenwood had told her about.

How did it come to Harry that there was another man there? Had he paused outside the door and heard them talking? Making love? His blindness must have been terrible then, not to know who it was, not to be able to see, and yet to be conscious that his wife was there in the bedroom, their bedroom, with another man. Carmichael hurt for him.

She came slowly downstairs and into the sitting room. She had no wish to go out and drive the Mini anywhere. Her eyes roaming round the room suddenly lit on a photograph in a silver frame on a small table by the window. Emily was smiling at her across the room. Emily's particular, rather superior, smile. Carmichael had a sudden desire to get up and smash the photograph on to the floor. She looked down at her hands and they were clenched so that the knuckles showed white in her lap.

"Don't be ridiculous," she thought. "He can't even see it." But she had to hold back the wish to smash the photograph.

Carmichael washed up the lunch things and at the required time switched on the oven. Then she laid the table for dinner.

Harry did not come back until after six and was profuse in his apologies. Carmichael greeted him in the hall, and he heard her footsteps.

"I didn't think I'd be as late as this, but more came up than I thought. You know how it is. I found when I really got down to it that the lecture was not as ready as I thought." He made towards his bedroom door. "I will go and do the necessary if you will test it for me."

"Yes, of course."

Carmichael was embarrassed though Harry seemed completely at ease and after a few minutes beckoned her into the bedroom and motioned through into the bathroom. Carmichael tested the urine, gave him the required amount of insulin, and then they both went back into the sitting room.

Harry Maitland got Carmichael a drink but did not pour one for himself.

"I wish you would tell me a little about your work," she said. "What is your lecture about? The one you're getting ready for now?"

"I don't think you'd be very interested. Castles, that's mostly my subject. Medieval castles and the reason they were stormed successfully, the position of the keep, and so on. When I was sighted, I went all over Europe examining and drawing plans. I wrote a book, which is still selling. It took a lot of doing, and of course I couldn't possibly do another." For once his voice sounded regretful. "The one I did is holding up very well. I put enough work into it, but these things need slight alteration from time to time. Other things are discovered." He suddenly sounded tired.

"I'm sure, I'm sure it must have been a lot of work, but I know you'll be able to do any alterations. You'll soon feel better again and able to do anything." Carmichael hated her voice and the rather nursy remark, but he seemed not to notice it.

Again the meal passed off quietly and easily. This time he filled her glass with red wine and Carmichael wondered how he knew when the glass was almost full. She didn't like to ask him, didn't like to make any reference to his dexterity. She couldn't make up her mind whether it was right or wrong to speak of his blindness. Maybe he liked to talk about it; she didn't know.

The evening, too, passed quietly, listening to music which Carmichael hardly understood but enjoyed because she was listening to it with him.

"Do you like music, Agnes?" he asked.

"Yes, I do."

"Do you like what we've been listening to—Mozart?"

"Yes, very much."

"That sounds heartfelt. I'm glad I've not been boring you with it. What time is it? I've left my watch in the bedroom." Carmichael looked at the clock.

"It's twenty past ten. I think it's time you were going to bed."

"In a little while. I think I'll break all the rules and have a cigar and a brandy. After all, it wasn't so bad, my test, was it? My doctor wouldn't like it and perhaps my nurse won't." Carmichael winced.

"I'm not your medical adviser. I'm not here in my capacity as a nurse." She said it almost abruptly and Harry turned to her quickly.

"I'm sorry. I didn't mean—"

"No. What I meant was that I wouldn't say anything, whatever you did." Carmichael tried to make it sound light and make him laugh.

His was a new laugh to Carmichael. How could she describe it? A sophisticated laugh, as if he were laughing at her because she was so naïve. Carmichael shrank back into herself as he got up and poured himself a small brandy. She refused another drink. He opened a box, took out a cigar, came back to the settee with it lighted, sat down again, but did not put on another record. Carmichael felt a sudden wish to get away.

"I'll clear the dining-room table," she said.

Something had gone wrong; the evening was deteriorating for some reason Carmichael couldn't tell. It was slipping, slipping away. Despair came over her. What had she done? Why wasn't she a brilliant conversationalist? Why wasn't she able to keep him amused while he drank his brandy and smoked his cigar?

She went into the dining room and carried some of the dishes and plates into the kitchen, feeling at the moment that this was the only role she had in this house—similar to Mrs. Greenwood's.

When she returned to the sitting room he had finished the brandy and had almost finished his cigar.

"I wonder how Mrs.—Emily's getting on? It must be over now, the exhibition."

"Yes, it probably will be—it's hard to say. It's not a proper exhibition, you know. Really just a gathering of friends to show . . . I believe they were going to have a little champagne party at the end of it, about half past six or seven. I hope it goes well. It's going to be a great disappointment if they don't understand the paintings or appreciate them. Emily's got a lot invested in this, if you know what I mean." He got up and went over to the music deck and switched it off. "It's time I went to bed, I think. Do you normally go to bed early?"

"Yes, I do usually. About now," Carmichael said.

He got up, brushed the front of his trousers down with his hand—in case there was any ash on them, Carmichael supposed, but there wasn't.

"Is the cigar butt out all right?" he asked and Carmichael looked into the ashtray.

"It's perfectly all right. Shall I check the windows or anything?"

"Did Emily tell you to? I bet she did. You know what I'm like," he laughed.

"She didn't. I didn't mean . . . ," Carmichael said and he laughed again.

"Oh, I wouldn't be offended if she had. I'm forgetful . . . Yes, do. Check the downstairs ones if you like." He stood at the table, looking towards her as she went round and found that all four windows were securely locked.

"Anything else I should do, like the back door or anything?" she asked.

Harry shook his head. "No, they're all right, but I'll have a check myself." He went through to the kitchen with sure footsteps and she heard him try the back door and then come back into the hall.

"I'll say good night, then," he said and at that moment they heard a key in the front door. It was thrown open and Emily Maitland stormed into the hall.

CHAPTER 17

"Emily, is that you?" Harry Maitland's voice was surprised.

"Yes, it's me. I've come back tonight. I just couldn't stand it. They were a crowd of morons. They knew no more about painting than they do down here. The remarks—I mixed with them —I shouldn't have. They didn't know I was the artist, of course. I won't repeat the remarks. I've got a raging headache. I've had a terrible day. The lighting was appalling. The champagne party was a disaster."

She sounded hoarse with rage, near to tears, and Harry put out a hand as if to take hers, but she avoided it.

"I'm going to bed. My head is truly awful."

She made for the stairs, not even looking in Agnes Carmichael's direction, but Carmichael determined to make her presence known.

"Oh dear, I am sorry. Would you like to get into bed and I'll bring you up something for your head. I'll make you a hot drink —would you like that?"

"Yes, I would. As a matter of fact I feel like being coddled for a change." Emily's bitter tone seemed to be directed against Harry.

"Very well. You go upstairs, have a bath if you want to, and I'll bring you up some hot milk."

"And some aspirin or codeine or something, for God's sake. My head's just thumping and I feel terrible."

She crossed the hall, ignoring Harry, and went straight up the stairs, her footsteps heavy, her face still furious.

"Oh dear," said Harry softly. "Oh dear. Things haven't gone well, I'm afraid."

"You go to bed. I'll look after her. I'll take her some codeine. I suppose you've got some in the bedroom or upstairs in the bath-room or somewhere?"

"There's bound to be some. She gets these heads when she's very upset. She takes things very hard."

Harry didn't appear to be particularly moved. Carmichael had been afraid that the scene in the hall would have upset him, but he seemed quite calm. He walked into his room, turning round and saying pleasantly:

"Good night, Agnes. I hope you have a good night, after you've ministered to Emily."

"If you want anything . . . Do you have a bell or some-thing?" Carmichael laughed and again he laughed.

"No, I haven't reached that stage yet. But if it were necessary, I could come out of my room and call you, I'm sure. Not that I shall need it. Don't worry."

Harry reassuring me, Carmichael thought glumly, as she watched the bedroom door close behind him and made her way up to her bedroom and sat on the bed and waited.

After some time she heard the bathroom door open and Emily making her way into her own bedroom.

"I'll get you that drink now." Emily Maitland did not look at Carmichael; just went to her dressing table and sat down and started to brush her hair.

Carmichael went downstairs, heated a cup of milk, took it upstairs, placed it on the small table on the landing, went into the bathroom, and opened the cupboard. Codis and aspirin. She took two Codis from the bottle, found a small medicine glass in the cupboard, put the Codis in, and took them in with the hot milk, putting them down beside Emily Maitland's bed.

Emily was now in bed, her beautiful hair spread about the pillow and on her shoulders. She rolled her head to and fro and put up a hand and clasped her forehead. She obviously wanted no communication with Carmichael. The ceiling light in the bedroom was on and Carmichael bent down to switch on the bedside lamp. Then, Emily spoke.

"It doesn't work. It's not the bulb; it's something else. I've asked Harry to get it seen to but of course he hasn't. Could you change it with the one over there?"

Carmichael looked across the room to where Emily pointed, on the other side of the bedroom. On the dressing table was another lamp. She went over and unplugged it, brought it to the bedside, and put it on the floor while she took the offending lamp away, wrapping the long flex carefully round the body of the lamp. Then she put the good lamp beside Emily Maitland's bed, plugged it in, and switched it on. She switched off the ceiling light. It made the bedroom appear in a softer, paler glow, suitable for someone with a bad headache. She took the broken lamp outside and stood it on the upstair hall table, then went back.

"Is there anything else I can do for you, Emily?" she asked.

"No, not at the moment. Thank you. My head's so bad—it was that blasted champagne. I drank too much of it; I felt so miserable. It was awful champagne, too. I won't want anything else. Once I get to sleep I'll be all right. I'll give you your cheque in the morning." Carmichael's heart almost stopped beating.

"Cheque?" she said. "What do you mean?"

"Why, to pay you, of course. You didn't think I expected you to look after Harry for nothing, did you? You will give him his insulin in the morning, won't you? I don't think I'll be in any state to get up early, and he has to have it at eight o'clock."

Carmichael stood by the bed. She could have struck Emily across the face. Emily's eyes were closed so she did not see Carmichael's expression.

"Yes, I'll give Harry his insulin in the morning. You needn't worry." Carmichael's voice was carefully controlled, quiet.

She crossed the room and turned back and looked at Emily, looked at the white, bad-tempered face, the closed eyes. She stood for a moment at the door, still looking, then went out closing the door gently behind her.

Having shut the door Carmichael felt she could not go along to the spare room, wash, undress, and get into bed and lie, looking into the darkness and thinking of those words, "I'll give you your cheque in the morning." She walked slowly down the stairs and stood again in the hall, looked across at Harry's door, then across at the sitting room. A light was still on in the sitting room. Of course, Harry wouldn't have known that. She was responsible for switching off the lights.

Carmichael's mouth twisted as she thought, That's my job— switching out the lights is part of what I get paid for . . . She could almost taste the bitterness in her mouth and feel it in her mind. She realized that she felt sick. She crossed the hall, went into the sitting room, and was about to walk across the room and put out the lamp but she didn't. She sat down on the settee, staring dully at the silver-framed picture of Emily.

Some minutes went by. Then she got up, went over to the picture, and gently with her forefinger traced the silver frame, rubbing it gently with her fingertips. It must have been taken sometime ago. Emily looked a lot younger—she was beautiful. Quite suddenly Carmichael picked up the picture and dropped it on to the floor. Emily's face still stared up at her. Dropping the photograph in its silver frame had made no sound on the thick carpet. She looked down at it and then, deliberately, she put her foot on it. As the glass cracked under the sole of her foot, she moved her foot forward and ground her heel into the photograph itself, obliterating Emily's face. She felt better. She left the photograph where it was, switched off the light, and went upstairs to bed.

CHAPTER 18

When Carmichael woke, the sun was streaming into her room and the birds were singing. She started up in bed—insulin, eight o'clock. Was she late? It had taken her a long time to fall asleep last night. She looked at the little travelling clock she had brought with her and put beside the bed. No, it was only ten past seven. Last night's scene came rushing into her head, but she dismissed it for the moment, got up, went into the bathroom, came back, and dressed.

She'd worn out last night's scene—worn it out, made it threadbare by going over and over it again. What next? This morning, at least, they would be together again; she would be with him for a little while longer. She went across the upstairs hall and put her ear against Emily's door. She could hear a faint buzzlike snore coming from the room. She smiled grimly to herself; perhaps another sign of age—snoring. She felt full of contempt for the aging woman, grabbing at any lover she could get—and probably having to pay to get even them. She grimaced and turned away from the door.

As she did so her eyes fell on the lamp, the broken lamp that she had stood on the table outside the bedroom the night before, the flex, the long, white flex, wound round and round, ready to be taken to the electrician or whoever was to mend it. She looked and an idea flashed into her mind with the speed of lightning, and she knew what she had to do.

She glanced at her watch. Twenty to eight. She'd plenty of time. She picked up the lamp, carefully unwound the flex, carefully and soundlessly. At the top of the stairs, just round the corner, was a socket to be used for a Hoover or a hall lamp. Carefully, Carmichael measured the amount of flex she would need to go across the top stair. Then, taking the plug, she carefully wound it round the wrought-iron bannister, and, having done so, she stretched the flex across the top of the stair and plugged it into the socket. She had measured carefully. It was taut and, because of the light carpet, almost invisible. She turned and looked at the lamp—that must be hidden. She moved it round the corner of the bannisters where the table on which it had stood partially hid it from view. Anyone coming out of the bedroom and going direct to the stairs would not notice it. She looked at her handiwork and nodded.

Now her mind felt empty—only the lamp, the flex, and the plug seemed real. She stepped over the flex, walked down the stairs into the kitchen, and there she made tea, sipped a cup herself, poured one for Harry, and took it to his room. To her surprise he was up, sitting on the side of the bed, dressed. She put the cup of tea down on the bedside table beside him, directing his hand towards it. As she did so, Harry put out his hand and touched hers. It was an ordinary gesture, just to thank her, but she thrilled to it. There was a chance, of course, that he still loved Emily, but Carmichael didn't think he could.

"Did you have a good night? Your step sounded very brisk."

"Yes, I did. I slept well," Carmichael lied.

"Good, I'm so glad, Agnes. I know you nurses listen if you have a patient, so don't sleep as well." She nodded, hating the remark.

"I'll fetch my tea in here." She went to the kitchen and fetched her cup and sat down in the chair opposite. He was still drinking his tea.

"I get very thirsty. That's how I know when my sugar is not quite right. You know that, of course."

"I know."

Agnes didn't want to enlarge any more on his illnesses—She wanted to savour sitting here in the intimacy of his bedroom. She finished her tea and Harry placed his cup on the bedside table.

"What time is it?"

"Insulin time." Carmichael's voice was light, easy. She felt suddenly as if she were young. She had put on a little of her perfume, and as she passed Harry she wondered if he noticed it.

Carmichael went into his small bathroom. It was lovely to be there amongst his shaving things, his after-shaving lotion; she smelled it with appreciation. She tested the specimen of urine he had placed ready for her, measured the required amount of insulin in the syringe, put back the insulin in the cupboard, and carried the syringe and the swab across to Harry. She bared his arm and it flashed across her mind that she hated to hurt him and almost couldn't bear to put the needle into his flesh. But that passed as she thought, He would die without it, and if he died, I would die too.

"Here it comes, just a little prick . . . that's what nurses always say, isn't it?" he said jocularly, but the remark hurt her.

"Yes, but I hope I won't hurt you," she said and drove the needle firmly home. Harry didn't even wince.

As she pushed the plunger in, there was a noise from upstairs; the bedroom door opening. A second or two and then there was a scream and a crash. Harry rose hastily to his feet as Agnes withdrew the needle from his arm.

"What was that?" Carmichael was just massaging the puncture with a swab. She lowered her hand.

"Good God! It sounded like someone falling down the stairs! It must be Emily. Emily—"

Harry walked quickly across the room, colliding with the jamb of the door. Agnes Carmichael followed him. Was she . . . ? Was Emily . . . ? Perhaps she had only broken her leg. She had screamed. One look was enough.

Emily Maitland lay at the foot of the staircase, her head at a very peculiar angle, one leg bent under her. She was wearing a pale blue nightdress over which was a matching negligée. It was rumpled round her. As they approached, she did not groan or stir. Carmichael concluded, with satisfaction, from the angle of her head, that she must have broken her neck. She, Carmichael, had gambled on that. Falling downstairs did not necessarily mean that one would be killed, but in this case she had been lucky.

"Emily, what's happened? Has she fallen?" Harry almost fell over the body of his wife, then knelt down beside it, feeling for her face. "Emily—Emily—what's happened, are you all right?"

"Harry, I don't think she is all right."

Agnes Carmichael was fearful as to what this disaster might do to Harry, but she was thankful she had given him his insulin. At least he had that safeguard. She watched him.

"I'll get a blanket," she said and she started up the stairs, remembering what was up there. Once there, she quietly took out the plug, making no noise in case Harry should hear her. She unwound the flex from the bannister, threading the plug quickly in and out. Then, just as rapidly, she wound the flex round the lamp, picked it up, and stood it gently on the hall table.

In Emily's room she grabbed the blanket from the bed and went back downstairs. She placed it over Emily's body—not over her face in case that would be too much of a shock to Harry. He couldn't be sure after all that Emily was dead, but he must guess. He was standing holding the telephone, talking. He must have dialled the doctor, Carmichael guessed.

"Yes, yes. She fell down the stairs. I've got a nurse here, a friend, but can you come at once? Please, Maurice. I'm so glad you're back. I thought you mightn't be. Yes, we will."

He came back unsteadily to where Emily lay and knelt down again. He was about to lift her head when Carmichael stopped him.

"I wouldn't move her, Harry, in case . . ." He nodded and gently stroked Emily's hair, which was something Carmichael hated to see.

"Thank God, you were here. Thank God, Maurice is back—that's the doctor. He's a friend and only lives just up the road. He won't be long."

At that moment the doorbell rang and Carmichael went and opened the door. The doctor walked in, bag in hand, and unceremoniously walked across the hall and knelt down beside Emily. He looked up and his eyes met Carmichael's.

"I'm afraid, Harry, I'm afraid, old man, your wife is dead. She couldn't have known much about it—she must have slipped and fallen head first down the stairs—a moment of fear perhaps, and that's all." He spoke intimately to Harry, like an old friend, and got up, clasped his hand, and gently drew him to his feet.

"Did you see this, nurse, did you see her fall?"

"Agnes—Nurse Carmichael—no, she was giving me my injection. Emily went away yesterday to her exhibition, you know, in London. It didn't turn out quite as she thought and she came home last night, but Agnes stayed on. Emily was worried about me being alone, so Agnes very kindly . . ."

"You didn't see her fall?"

Carmichael shook her head, and before she had time to speak Harry went on.

"No. Miss Carmichael was just giving me my injection when we heard this awful scream and the crash. She screamed, didn't she?"

Harry looked across to Carmichael, who nodded and said, "When she came home last night, doctor, she was rather upset. She went straight to bed and I took her something for her headache—she said she had a violent headache. I gave her two Codis and a glass of hot milk."

"What time was this?" the doctor asked.

"Oh, about half past eleven, I suppose. Somewhere about that time. I found the Codis in the bathroom cupboard and I dissolved them for her, but that couldn't make her . . . could it?" Carmichael was now pulling herself together. The shock for her had been, not Emily, but what the death of Emily might do to Harry. She looked at him and was reassured. His colour had returned.

"No, I don't expect so, but I suppose we'll have to inform the police." Harry made a movement as if to . . . and the doctor continued. "I'm afraid we'll have to, old man."

He went over to the phone, picked it up, and dialled a number and Carmichael led Harry back into his bedroom.

"Would you like to lie down for a little, Harry?" she asked him, but he wouldn't.

"I can't believe it, Agnes. Do you think the headache . . ."

"I don't know, Harry, I simply don't know. She might have been giddy or something."

"She drank too much; I was always telling her. She might have had a bit of a hangover this morning. But I'm not going to say that, Agnes, not about her. I can't."

Carmichael moved nearer to him and put her arm round his shoulders. For a second his head rested against her and she held him tightly.

"Thank God, you were here," he said again and Carmichael felt as she had felt before in similar circumstances, that what she had done was right and proper and that someone would benefit by what she, Carmichael, had put right.

She got up and walked firmly back into the hall, pulling Harry's door to, so that he could sit for a moment in private. The doctor looked at her.

"They won't be long, the police." He looked at the door and then said very quietly, "They'll take her straight away to the hospital morgue. Heavens what a thing to happen! She was always so full of life."

"Yes, it must be a shock for you, doctor. You were a friend of theirs, I understand."

"Yes, my wife and I have known them for years. I knew them when Harry first . . . when his sight began to go. Sad, very sad, hard to believe. We see death all the time, don't we, but when it's sudden like this, someone so vibrant . . . You're at the local hospital?" Carmichael nodded again.

"Nursing Officer," she said briefly and she thought he looked at her with more interest.

"Oh, I see, I didn't know that. I thought perhaps you were doing private work and had come here because Emily was away. She worried about him when his diabetes became unstable, as it is now—He refused absolutely to go back into hospital to be stabilized, especially as he was doing a course of lectures. I didn't realize you were a friend of theirs."

"Oh yes, I'm a friend," said Agnes firmly. After all, she could safely say that now and, she thought complacently, there would be no cheque to turn her from a friend into a paid servant.

CHAPTER 19

Carmichael and the doctor walked through into the sitting room and stood uncertainly looking at each other.

"They won't be long—the police. They'll have to bring a plainclothesman, a C.I.D. chap, I suppose, necessary but unpleasant for Harry. Still, it's a good job you're here."

Carmichael felt suddenly as if her legs were going to give way under her; her head felt light, her body cold. She sat down. As she did so, she noticed the broken picture on the floor. She must get rid of that. She hoped the doctor didn't notice it, but he moved away and stood facing the door, his back to the broken glass and the silver frame. Summoning the strength back into her legs, Carmichael rose.

"Excuse me."

She went through into the kitchen, and looked into several cupboards until she found a dustpan and brush, went back into the sitting room, bent down, and brushed the glass round the photograph and its silver frame, then picked that up, and put it in the dustpan as well. The doctor turned and looked at her curiously, attracted by the tinkling sound of the glass as it went into the dustpan.

"What's that?" he asked.

"Just a wine glass. Harry knocked it down last night and broke it."

Carmichael put the brush over the photograph in the pan so that the doctor could not see the scarred, mutilated face of Emily in the photograph. She took the debris out into the kitchen, searched around until she found a plastic bag, took the frame with its torn picture out of the dustpan, looked at it for several seconds, dropped it into the plastic bag and emptied the glass after it, tying up the top of the bag firmly. She unlocked the back door, looked around, and saw the dustbins. She took the lid off one and dropped the plastic bag into the bin—the last of Emily, she thought, smiling.

When she came back into the kitchen, closing the back door behind her, she heard the sound of a car outside the front door and thought, with a sudden sick feeling, police?

As she walked through into the hall, the doctor was opening the front door. Harry's door opened too and he came out. It was the police, one in uniform and one in plain clothes, as the doctor had predicted. Carmichael caught a glimpse of the car outside and a policeman sitting at the wheel. The two came in, nodding familiarly to the doctor. The man in plain clothes spoke to Harry.

"I'm sorry, sir. What happened?" They looked down at the body and then the C.I.D. man continued.

"Professor Maitland, isn't it? I'm very sorry, sir, very sorry. A terrible thing to happen. I'll have to ask you some questions, of course." As he said this, he removed the blanket and exposed Emily's face, the twisted neck. He replaced the blanket.

Harry led them through into the sitting room and they all sat down, the four men and Carmichael. For some moments Carmichael was asked nothing. They did not speak to her and she watched the four of them. She felt way above them, as if she were looking down at them and they were small puppets, playing as she pulled the strings. It was a nice feeling. If only they knew . . . But of course they would never know; she was much, much too clever for that.

The questions went droning on, to Harry Maitland, to the doctor. They would reach her, of course, eventually, but she didn't mind. She could tell the truth—she was just giving the injection when they heard the scream and the crash.

Upstairs, she visualized in her mind the lamp standing so innocently on the table. Perfect—perfect. At last, the policeman, writing busily in his notebook, looked at Carmichael, as the plainclothesman, having finished with the doctor and Harry, started to ask her for her version of the tragedy.

The questions were so simple. Carmichael answered them with composure and with ease.

"And you were just giving the injection when—"

"That's right," said Carmichael. "I was just giving the injection when . . ."

After the police had finished, the ambulance came. Within minutes they had Emily's body on a stretcher, covered from head to foot with a blanket, and strapped on. Emily was certainly neatly parcelled up, thought Carmichael.

But it was not nice, this; not nice for Harry. He couldn't see, of course, what they were doing, but he could hear and he could guess. Carmichael watched his face, then skirted round the ambulance man, and went and stood by his side and put her arm through his. The doctor was shepherding the body out of the door when Carmichael whispered. "They're taking her away. It's better, really it is."

Then she wished she had said nothing, for Harry Maitland turned to her sharply, "Better, better—what do you mean? Emily killing herself better?"

Again Agnes bitterly regretted saying the wrong thing. She had meant in her heart that he was better without her, but she had to reconstruct what she had said and she did so.

"I mean that it's better for you that poor Emily's body should not be here, don't you think?"

She felt his arm relax a little and he said, "I see. But I don't know that I want to hurry her out. She loved this house, she loved coming down those stairs. When we had a party she always made rather an entrance. She was a beautiful woman."

The regret in his voice stung Carmichael, but she remained silent. She was afraid that if she spoke, she might say something wrong again.

"I shall go with her of course, Maurice." Harry made as if to walk to the door, but the doctor turned round.

"I wouldn't, Harry, not at this juncture. They'll want you a bit later. I'm afraid there'll have to be an inquest, you know." The doctor's voice was kind, sympathetic, friendly and Harry Maitland reacted to it, but maintained his resolve.

"Yes, of course, but I want to go with her now. I don't like the thought of her going alone, Maurice."

"She doesn't know, she doesn't know," said Carmichael softly.

"She might. We don't know that. Perhaps that sounds ridiculous, but surely I can go to the hospital with her? Would you take me, Maurice?" He put out his hand to the doctor and Carmichael's heart sank, she felt him slipping away from her.

"If you want to, of course. Do you want a coat or anything?"

"No, no. If you'll bring me back, Maurice. Are you busy? I don't want to take up your time or keep you from patients."

"No, of course not. I'll take you there and bring you back, if it will make you feel better." He turned to Carmichael, "Will you stay here?"

Carmichael shook her head. "No, I'll come as well. I'd rather."

The doctor looked slightly helplessly at Harry, but Harry's face expressed nothing. Carmichael watched the two men. She was not going to be pushed into the background. She was not going to be made to feel the nurse who would wait at home until the patient came back with the doctor while she got him some breakfast. She thought of the insulin and mentioned it to the doctor, who nodded.

"I've got glucose in the car," he said.

Harry Maitland and the doctor got into the front seat of the car, Carmichael in the back, as the ambulance was disappearing out of the gate. They followed it. It didn't go fast and no siren sounded. Emily would not need haste or a siren now. Carmichael felt thankfully the old feeling of complacency and quietness and confidence settling back on her. In the back seat, she watched Harry's head lovingly. He was hers now. There was nothing between her and Harry except that body, and that would soon be gone.

Once he got over the initial shock, he would start thinking, thinking of the kind of woman Emily had been—her drinking, her impatience, her boyfriends. It would all come back to him, she was sure. The latest one, Jeremy, would probably ring up—after all, he didn't know. If Mrs. Greenwood was right and Harry had found them—or if not Jeremy, another man in bed with his wife—how would Harry react? Her hands clasped in her lap as the car sped along, driving behind the ambulance.

This was new to Carmichael: she'd never driven to the hospital behind an ambulance to go and report to someone. She wasn't quite sure who it would be—the front hall porter or someone in Casualty? Or the Casualty Sister, even? She couldn't remember exactly what happened when a body was brought in dead. When they arrived at the hospital she sat in the car and waited.

For some reason she didn't particularly want to be seen or recognized, though of course it would be nice to be addressed in front of the doctor and Harry as "Miss Carmichael," with the respect that they showed Nursing Officers. The ambulance drew up to the Casualty entrance. The doctor parked his car in one of the places outside the hospital reserved for visiting doctors. He put his hand on Harry's arm.

"I'll go in. You wait here a minute, old chap. I don't think this is awfully wise."

Harry Maitland nodded. Carmichael was sure he could hear the ambulance door open, hear the trolley being racketted down the slope. She suddenly leant over and wound up the window that the doctor had left open. Harry was quick to sense this.

"Open it, please, Agnes," he said, sharply. "I want to hear—after all, I can't see." Carmichael reopened the window. Another mistake, she thought.

"Do you want to get out and go in?"

"I'll wait and see what Maurice says, if you don't mind."

At that moment the doctor came out and poked his head in the window of the car. "There isn't much you can do, old chap, but if you do want to come in—"

"What would you do? Perhaps I've been a fool to come—I don't know. What would you do, Maurice?"

"Well, they'll take Emily into the—they've got to do that—later she'll be put in the Chapel of Rest. Then you can come. I think it would be wiser—but I'll go and ask, see if they want you —How's that? You stay there."

Carmichael came out of the back of the car and came round to where Harry, who had also got out, stood. She did not touch him now. She felt, sadly, that for the moment he was alienated from her. The way he had spoken about the window—sharply. It was not like him. She must not offend or cross him now.

Everything depended on her relationship with him now. She stood beside him, knowing he would sense her being there and put out his hand—put out his hand to her if he needed her. She prayed he would, but he made no such gesture.

The doctor was a few minutes gone and during that time Carmichael neither moved nor spoke.

"They say it will be better if you came back this afternoon. It really would be better." The doctor said this very gently to Harry, and Carmichael nodded in response to his voice.

"All right. What time?" Harry Maitland's voice was toneless.

"About three, they said. Then you can go to the chapel and see her."

Harry Maitland nodded and began to feel for the door of the car. Again Agnes would not touch him. He got in with the doctor, who waited for the ambulance to back away. Agnes Carmichael got into the back of the car and sat there miserably.

The crackling of words on the radio in the front of the ambulance were just discernible, though the words were unintelligible. Carmichael knew it would soon be called away to something else. For the ambulance men, Emily Maitland was already in the past. This for some reason gave her a feeling of reassurance and she relaxed a little against the upholstery of the doctor's car. The tension she had been feeling after Harry's sharp remark to her had been terrible. She realized she must make allowances for him. After all, Emily had been his wife, no matter how she had treated him.

Back at the house the doctor quickly took his leave.

"I must go now, Harry. I've got one or two calls I must do or I'd stay with you."

"There's no need. I'll be all right," Harry said.

The doctor, remembering Harry's condition, said, "You've had your insulin?"

"Yes, I was giving it, when—," said Carmichael.

"Well, you'd better have something, old man, you know you'd better."

"I'll stay with Harry and see that he has some glucose if he doesn't eat. I'm quite used to diabetics." Again Carmichael was certain she'd said the wrong thing, that she'd got back into the role of nurse.

"All right, I can leave that to you, then. Will you be staying for the rest of the day?"

"There's no need—," Harry started to say but Carmichael cut in quickly and determinedly.

"Yes, I will, I will indeed, I'm not due back at the hospital until tomorrow morning."

She said the words very firmly and the doctor nodded. Even although he was a friend of Harry's, Carmichael could see that he was slightly relieved that the responsibility would be taken over by someone else while he was away.

"Right." Even so, the doctor seemed half reluctant to go. "You're sure you're all right? I'll call in this evening. As you're going to the hospital this afternoon, perhaps Miss Carmichael will go with you—"

Harry cut in. "Thanks, Maurice, thanks for all you've done."

The doctor shrugged his shoulders and then realized that Harry could not see the gesture, as Carmichael did so often when she nodded. He said, "All I've done . . . what could I do, what could I do? I'm so very sorry, Harry." He stretched out his hand and clasped Harry Maitland's arm.

For a moment Carmichael thought that Harry was going to break down, but he straightened his shoulders and said, "After the initial feeling of terror, she wouldn't have felt anything, would she? Are you sure?"

"I'm sure." The doctor's voice was kind.

Carmichael thought, He's a nice man, but then Harry would have nice friends—that was what he deserved, not a wife who would let him down. Carmichael's hatred of Emily obliterated any pity she might have felt for the woman's death. She wouldn't have cared if she had suffered, if she had felt more than a moment of panic as she fell headlong—she hoped she had. Harry was well rid of her, well rid of her.

Suddenly, as Carmichael stood there in the hall, it was as if a picture of Emily flashed across her mind as she had been on the evening Carmichael had come to the house to be taken out to dinner. Carmichael saw her again walking down the stairs in her black evening dress, her smooth shoulders, her breasts swelling under the material of her dress—walking down the stairs as if she were making an entrance onto a stage. Carmichael remembered—she remembered that evening and then stopped herself . . . but not before she had seen again Emily's extended fingers holding the pound note toward the boy cleaning the hotel carpet. Well, Emily was good at doing the right thing, or had been, but when it came to a trip wire—Carmichael was smiling and not realizing it. She noticed the doctor looking at her curiously.

"Good-bye, nurse. I expect I shall see you again. I beg your pardon—I shouldn't call you nurse; it's Miss Carmichael." Carmichael nodded and the smile on her face disappeared, but not before the doctor had seen it. Carmichael could tell by the look in his eyes that he was puzzled by her expression, but he said no more and Carmichael softly closed the door, behind him.

CHAPTER 20

Harry Maitland and Carmichael stood in the hall, listening. They heard the slam of the doctor's car door, the engine start up, and the receding noise as it made its way out of the front gate and down the road.

"He's a grand chap. He's always been so much help to me."

"We must be practical, Harry. Though this dreadful thing has happened, we must still be sensible," said Carmichael. "I'm worried about your insulin and you having eaten nothing—nothing at all."

Harry shook his head impatiently. "You can't expect me to eat anything, for God's sake." Again there was that sharp note in his voice that Carmichael dreaded.

"No, no, of course not, but I'll mix you some glucose. Perhaps you could manage to take some, could you? I mean, you don't want to get an insulin—"

"No, I suppose not. This bloody disease."

Quite suddenly Harry sat down on the hall chair and covered his face with his hands. Carmichael thought he was going to cry. She hoped he would, so that she could put her arms round him. But he only sat there and said, "Yes, go and mix me whatever you think. I'll take it. I don't want, as you say, to go into an insulin coma—that would be the last straw. I want to phone someone."

Carmichael felt that she must expect this sharpness and tolerate it, wait till it passed and he became his usual courteous, gentle self, wait till the realization got through to him how much she loved him. And, she hoped, then he would learn to love her. She walked away from him into the kitchen. As she did so, she heard him lift the telephone, the slight ping of the bell. She heard him dialling the number easily and surely as if he knew it well. As she opened the kitchen cupboard looking for glucose which she was sure would be kept there, she wondered whom he was phoning.

She found the glucose, measured some out into a small glass and mixed it with water. This, just a small dose, should keep the insulin at bay. She knew, and had seen, what an insulin coma could be like—this was the last thing she wanted for him, the anxiety, the sweating. She mixed the glucose quickly and came back into the hall. Harry was speaking on the phone, so she stood beside him, holding the small glass in her hand, waiting.

"I can't believe it myself. I'm sorry to have shocked you like this . . . I know you were . . . I know . . . She was, I can't tell you how I feel . . . Yes, I know you will. Can you come? I want to see you. I'm going to the hospital this afternoon . . . Yes, if you would, that would be wonderful. I'd like that . . . About quarter to three then? Thank you."

He put the phone down and turned to Carmichael. "That was a friend. I need someone this afternoon to go to the hospital with me. I expect I shall have to talk to someone . . . I don't know . . . but this friend—"

"Drink this," Carmichael said quietly, putting the glass into his hand. Her heart was beating fast. This friend—she didn't want this friend. But she supposed it was a man friend, probably someone from the University whom he knew well . . . But she had wanted to go to the hospital, she had wanted to see Harry through this crisis, so that he would always remember that she had been there.

"I could have come with you. I could have driven you. I've got the Mini here and I know the hospital. Don't you think it would be better if I—?"

Harry drank the liquid and put the glass down beside the telephone and said firmly, "No, Agnes, I would rather not, I would rather go with this friend, if you don't mind. You've done so much already and I can't impose on you further."

"Impose on me! Harry, of course you're not imposing on me, but I quite understand. I'll stay the rest of the day, if you don't mind, because of your insulin." Harry nodded and there was resignation in the nod.

"That's very kind of you," he said absently. "I'll go and lie down, if you don't mind. I feel a bit . . . What you've given me is enough to stave off the affect of the insulin for the moment, isn't it?" He sounded infinitely weary.

"Yes, but I wish you'd try and eat something a little later, before you go to the hospital, even if it's just soup, toast . . . Whatever you say, I'll get it."

Again Harry nodded, but he seemed distant, far away. "Yes, I'll try, but if you don't mind, I'd like to be alone now. If you want to go—"

Carmichael felt as if she'd been cut with a sharp knife. "Of course I don't want to go. I'm staying here with you."

Harry frowned, but said nothing. Carmichael was not sure what the frown meant, but she put it down to fatigue and strain. He walked away from her, into his bedroom, and shut the door firmly behind him.

Carmichael found that she was trembling. The incidents of the morning were now crowding in on her. Emily's fall, the doctor, the police, the journey to the hospital, Harry's reaction, her feeling of responsibility towards him—all came pouring back on her. She felt, for a moment, that she'd like to be back safe in her own flat with Tibbles, preparing her Sunday lunch, thinking of tomorrow and duty, going into the hospital at nine o'clock, happy in her job. She wished again that she had not met Harry. She felt a foreboding that much unhappiness lay before her. Then, she shook herself. What nonsense . . .

Now, he would learn to rely on her. After all, what better for a blind diabetic than a nurse for a wife and a constant companion, watching over him, watching his health. She would not put herself forward too much, she wouldn't take away his independence, no. But she would not be like Emily—she would be faithful, not be impatient about things he forgot.

He would be so dear to her and she to him. Of course, she was glad she had met him. On a sudden impulse she went through into the sitting room and up to the bar cart, poured herself a brandy, and went and sat on the settee and sipped it, her face expressionless. She looked at the place where the photograph in its silver frame had stood. Surely, she thought, the ingenuity, the bravery she had shown this morning could not—would not —be wasted.

CHAPTER 21

At twenty to three Carmichael heard the front doorbell ring. This would be the person who was going to the hospital with Harry—twenty to three, the right time so as not to hurry him. She was about to leave the kitchen where she was trying to plan tonight's evening meal when she heard Harry open the front door.

Carmichael stood immobile, not wanting to appear to interfere, to seem to be overpowering him with attention. She knew she had got to treasure, to foster the independence that was so dear to him, but she could not resist going quietly out of the kitchen into the hall to see the friend Harry had telephoned.

It was a woman who came through the front door into the hall. She had been certain it would be one of his male colleagues. She, in her own mind, she, Carmichael, was the only woman friend she thought he had. Then she realized how ridiculous this thought had been. She looked at the woman who came in, put her arms round Harry, and kissed him on the cheek. She was middle-aged, white-haired, beautifully dressed, slim, tall, elegant. Another Emily? No, she had no arrogance. Her expression was composed, but her look at Harry, tender and sorrowful. As the woman's arms remained for a second or two holding Harry tight, Carmichael felt the old bitterness.

"Darling, oh, my poor darling, how did all this happen? If only she'd stayed in London with me. She didn't like what they said about her paintings, but . . . if only . . ." Harry did not answer, but Carmichael saw him clutch the woman's hand and remain silent for what seemed to her minutes but could only have been seconds. At last he spoke.

"It was dreadful, Margaret," he said. "She came back last

night. I didn't expect her. She was upset, very. Well, you know Emily—how sensitive she is—was—about her paintings."

The woman nodded and put her hand up and stroked the back of Harry's head like she would a child, comforting. Carmichael hated that hand so much she could have cut it off.

They both went through into the sitting room, Harry's arm still round her shoulders. He was leaning on her, leaning on her for the support that Carmichael wanted to be the only one to give him. She could do nothing but walk behind them. She would not, she was determined, leave them alone.

"Oh, I'm so sorry," Harry turned, hearing her footsteps and taking his arm from the woman's shoulders, he said, "This is Agnes, Agnes Carmichael, a friend from the hospital. She's been so kind. Emily was worried about leaving me with my diabetes unstable, and Maurice was away. He didn't get back till last night, so Agnes very kindly came and stayed. She was here when . . . she's been so good. Agnes—Margaret; Margaret Tarrant—Agnes Carmichael."

The two women shook hands, Margaret's was warm and firm, and Carmichael knew that hers was limp, clammy.

"Would you—can I get you a cup of tea or anything before you go?" Carmichael felt herself reverting to the role of servant, but what could she do, what could she say in front of this beautiful, elegant woman, who shook her head and gave her a charming smile, her eyes crinkling a little as she did so.

"No, thank you. It's kind of you but in a few minutes we're due at the hospital. That's what we've got to do, isn't it, darling?"

"Darling"—the word seared Carmichael as if she'd been burnt. But then, she thought, as she turned back to go into the kitchen, the only place at the moment where she felt safe, this kind of person always calls everyone "darling." "Darling" means nothing.

She heard them go into the hall, cross it, the front door shut, the car start. They had forgotten to say good-bye to her, but then, what was there to say? She was only . . . They would be back. Margaret would come back with Harry, she was sure, after they'd spoken to the doctor or whoever at the hospital they had to see. They would bring back Emily's things. Well, she herself would be back in the hospital tomorrow at nine. But she was determined that Margaret would not make her leave the house tonight. She would stay with Harry whatever happened. It would make their friendship more solid. She would spend as much time with him as she could, make her mark on him, make him realize how indispensable she was.

Margaret. Margaret what? Tarrant? Yes. She felt this woman might usurp her. She wondered whether the relationship between her and Harry was of long standing? This obviously was the friend of whom Emily had spoken, who had gone to London with Emily. Well, that would mean she was friendly with both of them. But then . . . the situation was too much for Carmichael, too much for her to work out. She couldn't understand it, so for the moment she left it and her mind started to revolve round the hospital, her flat, Tibbles, Mrs. Jenks, anything to keep out of her mind the picture of Harry and his look of immense joy at greeting Margaret.

Carmichael went back to wondering what she should do about the evening meal. He must have something, even although it was only this morning that Emily died. She must get something ready for him. After all, he was diabetic, he must eat —that was what she would have to look after for the rest of her life and she must set the pattern now. His insulin and then his meal, or if he couldn't eat, then glucose. She wondered if Maurice, the doctor, would come again and half hoped he would. But then, she was capable of testing Harry's urine, giving him the right amount of insulin. If she was in doubt, she could always ring the doctor and check. Yes, she suddenly felt again master of the situation. After all, Margaret Tarrant was not a nurse.

She looked in the freezer. Chops—well they'd have to do. She took out two and put them by the side of the sink to let them thaw. Then her eyes turned to the vegetable rack. Yes, she would prepare . . . she could, of course, boil potatoes and mash them with a little of the top of the milk—measure out so much for Harry. That's how she did it for herself, so why couldn't she do it for him? He could have a little more potato than usual considering how little he'd eaten today. He was sensible; he

knew his complaint. Perhaps he would feel a little better after
the visit to the hospital, seeing Emily there. Carmichael suddenly began to feel less anxious. She turned to the task in hand,
putting the faces of Harry, Margaret, and Emily out of her mind
and concentrating on what she was doing.

Mrs. Greenwood would be back tomorrow morning, before
she left for the hospital. Yes, she would certainly have to see
Mrs. Greenwood, relieve Harry of the awful task of telling her
about Emily. Yes, that was the reason for staying, a good reason
—but then, did she need a reason? She knew, in her heart, that
she did. She needed it because Margaret was there now. She had
Margaret to think of as well. Margaret . . . would she stay?
No, of course not, she'd go home. After she'd brought Harry
back she would go home, Carmichael was sure. He would have
to rest; she'd insist. She, Carmichael, would insist that he went
and rested on his bed, and Margaret, well . . . the thought of
telling Margaret what to do . . . Carmichael somehow could
not picture herself doing this; Margaret looked so capable, so
sure of herself.

A sweet for after dinner. She looked again in the refrigerator
and saw unsweetened yoghurt. That would do; with a little
cream that would be all right. She took out one for herself and
one for Harry, then put them back—they should be served cold,
surely? Then she wondered, in what she should serve them? At
home she ate yoghurt straight out of the little plastic container,
but that would not do here.

The crockery in the cupboard was superb—the dinner plates
white with a red and gold band. She turned one over and read
ROYAL MINTON. Everything in this house was beautiful—pictures, china, glass, silver, everything was beautiful. And now
something else beautiful had entered it—Margaret Tarrant.

Carmichael leant for a moment on the edge of the steel sink.
She had not realized how much this day had taken out of her.
She found herself trembling, but she would not falter. She
would make Harry's life happy, healthy, and he would learn to
love and rely on her.

She turned again to the vexed question of the vegetables.

CHAPTER 22

Four o'clock came and there was no sign of Harry or Margaret Tarrant. Five o'clock, six o'clock . . . Surely, they'd come straight home? Perhaps Margaret had taken him back to her house? At about twenty past six Carmichael heard the key in the lock of the front door and she went joyfully out into the hall, hoping that Margaret would just drop in, then suggest that Harry might like to rest, and disappear. Nothing like that happened.

Harry came in. He looked better but tired. Margaret Tarrant followed him, carrying in her hand a small suitcase. She looked at Carmichael, smiled, then crossed the hall and went up the stairs, still carrying the suitcase. There was an intimacy apparent in her movements in the house, as if she knew where everything was and knew exactly where to put the things she was carrying in the suitcase—Carmichael presumed that they were Emily's.

Carmichael spoke, to let Harry know that she was there; she had been standing there so quietly.

"Oh, Agnes. I'm sorry, I wasn't attending."

"How was it, Harry?" Carmichael asked.

He must have sensed the deep concern in her voice because he turned to give her his full attention. "It was rather dreadful. We went into the Chapel. Margaret said Emily looked very peaceful, not a mark at all on her face, thank God. She wouldn't have liked to have been marked. She hated blemishes."

He stopped suddenly and turned away from Agnes Carmichael and walked into the sitting room.

Margaret came down the stairs and followed Harry, smiling at Agnes as she passed her, and then looking back and asking her, "Is it all right if Harry has a little brandy? I must ask his medical adviser, mustn't I?" She smiled and her voice was friendly and warm.

"Yes, indeed. I've got a meal ready." She followed them.

"Oh, how very thoughtful. Of course Harry must have something, because of the . . ." She looked enquiringly at Carmichael.

"Strangely enough, I feel a bit hungry now," Harry said. "Since we've been there and you said she looked so serene, I feel better in a way. Slightly detached from it. I think perhaps it hasn't really hit me yet."

Margaret sat down beside him and slipped an arm through his and clasped his hand, the hand that Carmichael so longed to hold in hers. Margaret sat with it cradled in her lap, holding his fingers in both her hands, rubbing the back of his hand softly with hers.

"Are you cold, darling?" she asked and he nodded, then straightened his back as if to admonish himself for a momentary weakness.

"Yes, I am a bit chilly, but it'll go off."

"That's because you haven't eaten anything all day. I'll light the fire."

The big, open fireplace was full of logs and Carmichael wondered for a moment how Margaret was going to light it. Then she noticed, in the basket beside the fireplace, partly concealed by logs, a gas cylinder. Margaret picked out the gas poker attached to it, lighted it, and thrust it under the logs. It looked as if she had done it many times before. Immediately the bark round the wood started to crackle, and although the room was already warm, it made it seem more cheerful. Harry relaxed as he heard the noise of the fire.

"Thank you, darling, it's not really cold in here. It's me, I suppose."

"Well, it's because you haven't eaten anything, as Margaret said." Carmichael's voice was bossy and nursy and again the soft, soothing voice of Margaret Tarrant cut in.

"That's true. When you haven't eaten, it makes you feel cold. I'm a little hungry now. What have we got for dinner?" It was kindly said, but Agnes Carmichael immediately felt like Mrs. Greenwood.

"I've got pork chops cooking and vegetables. Is that all right, Harry?"

He jumped as she spoke his name and said, "What did you say, Agnes? I'm so sorry."

"She was just saying that she's got dinner ready for us. Isn't that nice of her?"

Harry nodded. "Agnes is so kind. I don't know what I'd have done without her when Emily fell. You were a tower of strength, Agnes."

Carmichael warmed a little at the words and they helped to dispel the dismay she felt at Margaret's remark, "She's got dinner ready for us." Carmichael had only put two chops in the oven; she'd got to get a third in without them knowing.

"Excuse me," she said and hurried back into the kitchen. She hastily took a third pork chop straight from the freezer, opened the oven, and popped it in, pushing the other two along the tin with a knife. She hoped that was how they liked them done—in the oven. Plates, she thought. She put three under the grill and turned it on, very low. What else? Wine? She suddenly felt her own complete inadequacy. Should you have white wine with pork chops? Where was the white wine? Would it be all right to serve it so soon after Emily's death? It wasn't, after all, a festive occasion, and wine, well . . . A dry white wine, she thought automatically, but what was a dry white wine? How did you know it by the label?

Carmichael bent down to see that the oven door was properly shut, then opened the refrigerator, and to her relief, a bottle of white wine, was in there, uncorked, with a silver screw top in it. She took the bottle out. It was over two-thirds full. Surely that would be enough. For the moment, she couldn't think any more. She must . . . She left the kitchen and went upstairs to the bedroom.

She combed her hair, tried to back comb it a little to make it look thicker, put some fresh powder on her face, a little more lipstick, and a tiny touch of her perfume. Then she came downstairs, and as she did so, she heard the strains of music, soft and beautiful, coming from the sitting room. She hesitated by the door. Harry was sitting on the sofa with Margaret still beside him, still holding his hand. One of them must have got up to put on the record, Carmichael thought, assuming it was Margaret. She had gone straight back and taken his hand again.

There was a brandy in front of Harry and another in front of Margaret. Harry's eyes were closed. Margaret looked up suddenly as she became conscious of Agnes Carmichael's presence. She looked towards her but didn't move.

"Soothing, Schumann, isn't it?" she said and Harry, thinking she was speaking to him, nodded and tightened his grip on her hand. Carmichael watched with dismay. Schumann. Yes, she'd heard of him, but she wouldn't know who he was unless they'd told her.

She went and sat stiffly in the armchair beside them, leaned back herself, and tried to listen appreciatively to the sound. The music went on and not a word was spoken; the fire crackled and Carmichael thought of the meal. She'd found in the freezer some frozen peas and some frozen green beans, they would have to do. She had peeled, cooked, and mashed potatoes with butter and milk and hoped that was right.

At last she got up, went back into the kitchen, opened the oven, and turned the chops. The vegetables were probably overcooked, but what could she do? She couldn't rush in there and say "Dinner's ready"—you didn't do things like that in this house. Indeed, how did you do them? She went through into the dining room and inspected the table. She was going to serve the yoghurt in the pretty little glass dishes she had found in the kitchen cupboard. She had taken the three yoghurts out of the refrigerator and put them in a row ready to be emptied into the dishes. She would have to do the serving, she supposed. She rushed back to the kitchen, opened more cupboards, found a vegetable dish, and put it in the oven. The chops now were practically cooked, so she turned the oven down. At home in her flat she served herself straight from the saucepan; but not here, of course. Suddenly, she longed to be back there, safe with Tibbles.

This sense of inadequacy she never felt when she was at the

hospital. Here she was out of her depth. The thought nearly overwhelmed her—that if she were to marry Harry now that he was free, even if she were to live with him, to love him forever, she must learn these things. Tonight, she knew, she had done many things wrong, but she could learn. She was certain she could learn.

She went out of the kitchen and listened. The music had stopped. They were talking quietly. She went across, opened the door, and looked tentatively at Margaret Tarrant.

"Oh, I'm so sorry, Agnes. We were lulled a little by the music, weren't we, Harry? I didn't ask if I could help you. Can I?" Carmichael shook her head.

"No, I'm just going to bring the chops in, if that's all right . . . ?" Servile again, she thought, but Margaret smiled her sweet smile.

"That's right. Just let's picnic. That's all we want. As long as Harry gets something to eat . . ." Carmichael made her way back to the kitchen and she heard Margaret Tarrant go through to the dining room. Carmichael brought in the vegetable dish, which had become very hot in the oven and she was using the oven cloth to hold it.

She crossed the dining room and Margaret said hastily, "Wait a minute," and went over to the drawer in the large sideboard which ran along one side of the room and took out a big, thick table mat and put it on the table, smiling at Agnes Carmichael as she did so.

"It's such a lovely dining table. We don't want to mark it. Emily was so proud of this table, she and Mrs. Greenwood . . ."

She stopped and Carmichael nodded dumbly, put the vegetable dish down, and went back to the kitchen, returning with three plates on a tray. Perhaps she should have put the chops on the flat silver dish she had seen in one of the cupboards and decorated it with parsley or something? Oh Lord, they'd just have to put up with it.

"I'll go and get Harry," Margaret said.

"No. Please sit down. You sit there and I'll fetch Harry." It was the first determined remark Carmichael had made since

Margaret Tarrant had come on to the scene and Carmichael noticed that she looked at her, slightly surprised but was obviously too well bred to make any remark. She sat quietly down where Carmichael had indicated.

Agnes came back into the dining room with Harry, her hand lightly touching his arm, but he needed no guidance now. Nothing from me, Carmichael thought, not yet anyway, but he would, he would. Perhaps after a time they would go away together. Margaret would go back to her own home . . .

The meal progressed in silence, Carmichael and Margaret helping Harry as they thought necessary, but Margaret so quietly, so gently, he responded always to Margaret's side of the table when he realized where she was sitting. It seemed endless. Harry played with his food, tried to eat.

"I've got a little more potato than usual," he said. He tried to smile at Agnes and she replied formally.

"Yes, you need a little more carbohydrates, you see, to make up . . ." She stopped. What did she say that for? There was no need for it. He knew. If she could only attain Margaret Tarrant's well-bred silence, her quiet peacefulness . . .

Carmichael collected the plates and took them into the kitchen, waving aside Margaret's offer to help her. She tipped the yoghurt into the glass dishes, found a small jug, put in some cream, and took it all into the dining room.

"Is this all right for Harry?" Margaret asked and a sudden flash of hatred came out of Carmichael's eyes which Margaret Tarrant obviously noticed with surprise.

"If it weren't all right, I wouldn't give it to him," Carmichael said.

Margaret said nothing. She did, however, make a slight grimace, as if to say, "Oh dear, I must be careful how I tread."

"Is that your car in the drive?" she asked, and before Carmichael could speak, Harry Maitland replied.

"Yes, that's Agnes' Mini." His fingers were feeling curiously round the glass dish in front of him.

"Oh, that's all right then," said Margaret. "I was going to offer to run you home." She had forgotten, or chosen to overlook, Carmichael's last sharp remark.

"I'm not going home tonight. I'm staying the night here with you, Harry. Margaret, I expect you'll be wanting to get back to your family. I shall be quite all right. I shall be able to give Harry his insulin and everything."

"Agnes, I'm not going to . . . I feel better, really. If I could take that this morning, well, surely . . ."

"There's your insulin in the morning. No, I must stay."

It was Margaret who broke in quietly. "Very well. Though, Agnes, I have no family to get back to, so you needn't worry about that. I live by myself; my children are grown up. I'm too old to have children still living at home."

It was lightly said, and she turned to Harry, "It's very sweet of Agnes to stay. She can give you your insulin in the morning and talk to Mrs. Greenwood and then I'll come round a bit later."

"Can you stay then? Can you stay when you come tomorrow?" Harry's voice was anxious and Margaret put out a hand and covered his.

"Of course I can, darling. You don't think I'd leave you alone in these circumstances. There'll be so much to arrange. I'll help you, you know that."

Harry relaxed almost at once, then picked up a spoon and again felt curiously the edge of the glass bowl in which Carmichael had put the yoghurt.

"Aren't these the finger bowls?" he said suddenly.

Margaret's eye caught Carmichael's. "Yes, darling, they are, but how was poor Agnes to know? She's never been in that kitchen before. I think they make quite nice sweet dishes."

"Oh, of course, how stupid of me. As you say, how could Agnes know?"

Carmichael's cheeks were flaming. She would make a mistake like that, she thought. But how was she to know? She'd never seen finger bowls before. Perhaps they should have had finger bowls with the chops, but she, Margaret, had said just a picnic. Oh God, she'd got such a lot to learn. She'd go to classes. She'd get a book on etiquette tomorrow. She was bad at introducing people, too. She would have to learn something about music.

She looked across at Harry, trying to ignore Margaret Tarrant's presence, trying to pretend she wasn't there. He was worth it, worth anything, any sacrifice, even the sacrifice of Margaret Tarrant, if that were necessary.

The evening dragged on, Carmichael calmed down a little. They sat for some time, but no more music was played. It seemed that Harry just wished to sit beside Margaret, his hand in hers.

Margaret had helped Carmichael take the dishes through from the dining room into the kitchen and piled them on the draining board, saying lightly, "Mrs. Greenwood can do these in the morning."

This had offended Carmichael. She felt she was in charge and it was she who should have said "Mrs. Greenwood can do them in the morning." After all, it was she who was seeing her, she who was staying, not Margaret Tarrant.

At last Margaret said the words that Carmichael was longing to hear.

"I'd better go, darling. You're tired and you'd better get to bed."

He stopped her and said, "Don't go. It's such a comfort to have you here."

When he said it, Carmichael felt as if a nail had been driven into her heart. However, Margaret Tarrant made her point and Harry accompanied her to the door. As it closed behind her, he sighed a deep sigh, then turned to Carmichael.

"She is such a wonderful person. She was fond of Emily and very kind about her painting. But then, Margaret is always kind. She's right, though—I am tired Agnes. I'll go to bed now and thank you for staying. It is very kind of you. I hope you're comfortable up there."

Carmichael felt that he would rather have had Margaret, and had she not been there, indeed Margaret might well have stayed. But Carmichael had won the battle so far.

"Do you need any help? Is there anything I can do for you? Get you?" she said, more guarded now. She was learning to respect his independence.

Harry shook his head. "No, thank you. I shall be all right. I don't want anything else. When the arrangements are finished"

—he hesitated, then went on—"when the arrangements are finished, I shall be glad to get back to the University, I really will."

"We'll have to see what the doctor says," said Carmichael, her brisk, nursy voice escaping by mistake. He nodded.

"Thank you again, Agnes, and good night."

Agnes was loath to see him go. "I'll bring you a cup of tea in the morning and do your test and give you your insulin before I go to the hospital."

He nodded and again said, "Thank you." He went into the bedroom and closed the door behind him.

How she would have loved to have been able to put her arms round him, cushioned his head on her shoulder, and say, "Don't worry. Emily wasn't worthy of you. You know she had her boyfriends. You know . . . she paid them . . . she was nothing. I will be everything to you."

She felt the words going round in her head as she stood there. She thought again, as Harry's door closed, of Margaret Tarrant, her serene face, her gentle, aristocratic voice, and she hated her.

CHAPTER 23

Next morning Carmichael came downstairs early. She was getting used to the house now. She went to the kitchen and made tea quickly and took it in to Harry at ten minutes to eight.

"Good morning. How are you feeling?" she asked him tenderly, trying to infuse into her voice all that she felt for him, but he hardly seemed to be listening to her.

He was sitting on the side of the bed in his dressing gown, feeling his Braille watch. "It's nearly eight, isn't it?"

He turned to her and went on, "Well, today is going to be another unpleasant day, but I've got to tackle it, haven't I?"

"Yes, I'm afraid you have, Harry, and how I wish I could be here with you and go to the . . . well, wherever it is you've got to go and help you with what you've got to do."

Harry nodded, absently. "Oh, that's kind of you, Agnes, but of course, Margaret will be here. She'll drive me."

Perhaps he sensed her feelings, for he suddenly added, "Not that you haven't been wonderful, you really have. I don't know what I'd have done without you, especially when . . ."

"I'll do your test and give you your insulin." Carmichael could not take advantage of the kind and thankful remark. She could not touch him as she wanted to, put her hand on his shoulder, and press it . . . In his small bathroom she tested the specimen he had left for her, measured the insulin, and came back with it.

The insulin given, there was nothing else for her to do. The touching of his flesh while she gave the injection was an unhappy touch, because it meant she had to hurt him and she hated that, although he was so used to the injection, he took it without flinching, without even remarking on it. He merely pulled the sleeve of his dressing gown down and thanked her.

As he did so, Carmichael heard a key in the lock of the front door.

"Ah, that'll be Mrs. Greenwood. I'll go and see . . ." Harry rose from the bed, but Carmichael broke in as he spoke.

"No, no, I'll tell her. Leave that to me." Was she being bossy again? She couldn't tell by Harry's expression.

He merely nodded impassively and said, "Very well."

Carmichael went through into the kitchen. Mrs. Greenwood was hanging her coat up on the door and she turned in surprise to greet Carmichael.

"You still here? I thought you'd have gone."

Seeing the look on Carmichael's face, she continued. "What's happened? He hasn't gone and died, has he? I mean, he hasn't gone into one of those comas? Oh, no." She looked genuinely distressed and Carmichael cut in, hastily.

"No, it's not Professor Maitland. It's Mrs. Maitland. She came home on Saturday night and on Sunday morning she came out of her bedroom and fell down the stairs, just as I was giving the Professor his insulin."

Mrs. Greenwood's jaw dropped. "Her? Not . . . she's not . . . ?" Carmichael nodded.

"Yes, I'm afraid so. She broke her neck. It's been a terribly distressing weekend for all of us."

"All of you? I should think a distressing weekend for her. Poor Emily, poor Mrs. Maitland. How did he take it? I wonder it didn't give him one of those comas."

"He took it marvellously, but then, he's a marvellous person, isn't he?" The words slipped out so fervently, before Carmichael could stop them, that she felt Mrs. Greenwood look at her curiously.

"Did the doctor come? What happened?"

"Yes, the doctor came. Luckily he was back. He came back the night before. The police came too, and they took her away in an ambulance. And then a Mrs. Tarrant came."

"Oh, Mrs. Tarrant. That's good. She's a lovely lady. She knew all about Emily and the way she was carrying on. She knew about it, but she was a good, loyal friend. I'm glad he's got her— that'll make all the difference."

"Yes, she was very kind," said Carmichael primly, "very kind."

"She's really great, that one. A real lady. They've always been great friends, very close." The look she gave Carmichael, Carmichael could not at first understand.

Mrs. Greenwood went on. "Well, poor Professor Maitland—as if he hasn't got enough on his plate with his diabetes and everything. Still, it was a good job you were here. Why didn't you go, though? When she came back, I mean?"

"Because I was asked for the weekend and because Mrs. Maitland wasn't very well when she came home. She had a headache. They didn't like her pictures and she . . . well, she wasn't in too good a mood."

"Oh yeah, I bet she had a headache. I bet she slopped up the champagne. She did drink a lot. Still, poor lady . . . I wouldn't have expected that to happen. I wouldn't wish that on a dog."

"Well, Mrs. Tarrant will be round shortly, she said she would come about nine or soon after," said Carmichael, and Mrs. Greenwood nodded and started to bustle round the kitchen, taking charge.

"I'll have to see about the food then. I'll have to get some lunch for him. Perhaps they'll be out having to go to the police or the hospital. Will they?" Carmichael didn't answer and Mrs. Greenwood rattled on. "Well, I'm used to doing the shopping. I'll get some things. I'll go and see the poor man and ask him. Well, I'll have to, won't I, and say how sorry I am?"

"He's dressing," said Carmichael coldly, and again Mrs. Greenwood looked at her—summing her up, Carmichael thought.

"Well, I'm sure he is, but he won't mind me. He's used to me, you know. I've been working for them for the last twenty years." It was an obvious rebuff. "What are the finger bowls doing out, then? Oh, they've been used for the yoghurt! What a scream! Who did that? Not Mrs. Tarrant . . ."

Carmichael didn't answer. She felt she had been wounded enough and it brought back last night and the humiliation of having done the wrong thing. People were always humiliating her, she thought, and she suddenly hated everybody. At that moment she hated Mrs. Greenwood most of all.

She turned on her heel and left the kitchen, saying over her shoulder, "I'll call in this evening and see that everything is all right. Will you please tell Professor Maitland that? I'm going."

"Oh, I expect Mrs. Tarrant will move in. She's bound to—she won't leave him alone."

Carmichael's heart sank at the words, but she knew they were probably true. Mrs. Greenwood knew the setup of the Maitland home far better than she did. Suddenly she felt she didn't want so see Harry again; she couldn't bear it. She went upstairs, packed her small suitcase, came down, went out of the front door, and got into the Mini. Before she drove away, she hesitated, wondering if she should speak to him again. But no—if she told him she was coming back this evening, he might stop her, so she wouldn't. She drove away, straight back to the hospital.

In a way, it was a relief to walk through the hospital doors into the domain she knew, and yet she felt different, disorientated, as if she were coming into alien surroundings—or was it from alien surroundings? Her mind felt curiously detached from both scenes.

It was as if at the weekend she had been in a play or seen it on television. She tried to rid herself of the feeling. It was of course ridiculous, but her flat and Tibbles seemed far away. She must put that right. She must go home at lunchtime instead of staying to lunch in the Canteen, collect Tibbles, put her back in her own flat, and thank Mrs. Jenks.

Johnson was sitting at her desk when Carmichael went in.

"Good morning," she said. "How I loathe Monday mornings and these bloody rotas. I dunno, I never seem to get one Sister who does them properly, do you?"

Carmichael shook her head, "There's usually one or two wrong, but not as many as when I first came. I've got them a bit better trained now." The remark helped Carmichael.

"Well, you don't seem to have as much trouble as I do," Johnson went on. "You must give me a tip. This one, Tyson ward—honestly, she's left herself with two nurses in the evening. Supposing one of them goes off sick? I know there's not much to do on that ward at night, but, really, it seems to me to be cutting it a bit thin. Of course, she's put the whole staff on for the morning round—you know her. Well, I'll have to go and talk to her later on." Johnson leaned back in her chair. "Let's have coffee early. I need it—I had quite a weekend. What did you do?"

"I stayed with the Maitlands."

"Oh." Johnson looked only mildly interested, then obviously felt she had dismissed it too quickly, and added, "I hope you had a nice time. Aren't they the people . . . The Professor? The blind man and his wife?"

Carmichael nodded, then she felt she must tell someone. "It was a dreadful weekend. Mrs. Maitland—Emily—came home from London on Saturday, instead of on the Sunday morning as we thought she would. Then, on Sunday morning, she got up and fell down the stairs and broke her neck—she was brought in here to the morgue. We've had an awful time." Carmichael was gratified to see Johnson drop her pen on her desk and look at her with wide eyes.

"No . . . how awful! What a good thing you were there! I mean, with him being blind. Do they have servants living in? I mean, somebody there with him?"

"No, only a daily woman. I was the only one there with Emily and Harry." She said the Christian names self-consciously. "I was just giving him his insulin when she fell."

"Oh, you were doing a bit of Private nursing were you, staying there? I see," said Johnson and Carmichael harshly contradicted her.

"I was not doing a bit of nursing. I was there as a friend. Mrs. —Emily did not feel very well when she came home, so I said I would give Harry his insulin next morning, and while I was giving it, she came out of her bedroom and fell." Carmichael, for a moment, relived the episode. She could feel again the driving in of that particular needle, the scream, and the crash.

"Well, how awful for you—not to mention him! What a weekend! I wonder you were able to come to work. I think it would have flattened me. I know you're a nurse, but when something happens outside the hospital, it's not the same is it? I found that one day when I was in the street and there was a car crash. Do you know there was a bleeding man staggering about the road and I felt completely out of my depth? It isn't the same as when you're in Casualty, where everything is to hand. You feel like a fish out of water, and when the St. John Ambulance man came, I felt he knew a hell of a lot more than I did. You must have felt like that too, did you?"

Carmichael shook her head, she was tired of Johnson's chatter. "I don't think I want to talk about it any more, Johnson, if you don't mind."

Johnson nodded quickly. "I'm sure you don't. It must have been pretty hairy. Let's forget it for the moment, eh? I expect he's got friends who'll come in and help."

"Oh, yes, he's got friends." The bitterness in Carmichael's voice made Johnson look at her fixedly and then hurriedly go back to checking the hated rotas.

CHAPTER 24

At lunchtime Carmichael drove round to her flat and went upstairs. Again she had a feeling of strangeness. It was as if she didn't know the place, as if she had not been here for years, as if the only place she knew in the world was the Maitlands' house. It was an odd feeling. She knocked on Mrs. Jenks' door, proffering her, as she took the cat in her arms, a little box of chocolates that she'd got from the shop trolley going round the wards this morning. She listened halfheartedly to Mrs. Jenks.

"Oh, you shouldn't have. Tibbles has been absolutely sweet—a lovely weekend guest, I call her. I wouldn't have minded having her longer, would I, my love?" Mrs. Jenks stroked the cat under the chin.

Tibbles was purring in recognition of Carmichael and rubbing her head against Carmichael's chin. She clasped the cat, she felt warm, furry, and happy, but her feeling for Tibbles was not quite the same. Nothing was the same. She thanked Mrs. Jenks again and walked across to her flat, the cat still in her arms.

She opened the door and walked in. The place seemed cold in spite of the fact that the radiator was on. The cat leapt out of her arms on to the glass top of the radiator, one of her favourite places, and gazed out of the window as she always did, quickly back to normal behaviour. Carmichael wished she could adapt as quickly.

She switched on the electric fire. The flat seemed so empty, so remote from her. She went through to the kitchen. Yes, there was bread in the fridge. She took out some slices and prepared herself cheese sandwiches for her lunch. She sat down in front of the electric fire, switching on the television. The sandwiches tasted of nothing and the television didn't seem to get through to her at all. She looked at the picture with apathy—the news—

but she didn't take any of it in. All she could think of was Harry.

She looked at the clock. Quarter past one. Would they be having lunch? Had they been to the hospital this morning? Would he have had to make a statement to the police? Wherever he had been, Margaret was supporting him. Carmichael wondered if the police would contact her. Probably not.

And Mrs. Greenwood. Mrs. Greenwood would have got the lunch for them, done the shopping, taken charge. Would Margaret Tarrant have moved in by now? Perhaps distributed her things round the bedroom, opened the wardrobe door . . . ? Suddenly Carmichael remembered. The green dress—her green dress—was still there, hanging up in the wardrobe in the Maitlands' spare room. She had forgotten it. The thought filled her with warmth—that something of hers was still in that house, faintly smelling, she hoped, of her perfume. Margaret Tarrant would move it aside and put her clothes near it, but that, even that, did not detract altogether from the feeling that something of hers was still in his house. It meant, also, an excuse for going back this evening.

She stopped eating her sandwiches. Not that she needed an excuse to go back, of course. When should she go? What time? Half past six—after they'd had their drinks? Then they'd be almost certain to ask her to stay to dinner, wouldn't they? Then she could give Harry his insulin—that was the excuse for going back. And now, the dress. How could they do anything else but ask her to dinner? She was not sure they would. But then, she would want to hear what they had done, what they had said about Emily, when the funeral was to be so that she could go. There were all kinds of things that she would want to talk about.

If only there had been a little more time—if only she had been there one or two weekends, not just those two nights. If only . . . The green dress hanging in the wardrobe in the spare room of Harry's house was a link. It made her feel better. She finished the sandwiches, made herself a cup of coffee, fed Tibbles, and then decided to shut her in until she got back. Then she thought, well, it might be late . . . Mrs. Jenks . . . She closed the door of her own flat and went and knocked on her neighbour's.

"Would I be putting you to too much trouble? A friend of mine died at the weekend and I've got to see to her husband. He's very upset. Would it be too much to ask you to let Tibbles out a little bit later? She's having her meal at the moment."

"Of course, my dear. If you want to stay away for the night, if your friend is very distressed, you do. I'll look after Tibbles."

"I don't think I will, thank you, Mrs. Jenks, but it would be kind of you to keep an eye on her. I would feel happier knowing Tibbles is not alone."

"Of course. I know what you mean. She can come in here as much as she likes. If she doesn't want to go into your flat with you not there, I've got the key and can let her in and out just as her ladyship pleases." Mrs. Jenks smiled her wide smile and Carmichael nodded.

"Thanks, thanks a lot. I don't want her to feel that she's deserted, you see."

Mrs. Jenks nodded again and Carmichael turned and went down the stairs thinking when eventually she managed to . . . when eventually she moved in with Harry forever, Tibbles of course would come too. She imagined the cat in that sitting room, curled up on that settee or on Harry's lap—she knew that he'd love her—herself sitting in the armchair, perhaps having put a record on, a record that by that time she absolutely understood. Perhaps he might like to hear some of hers . . . *The King and I* . . . but somehow she doubted it. Musical appreciation classes—that would be the next thing. Yes—and a book on etiquette. She would buy it, not get it from the library. She would get it, if possible, on the way back to the hospital today. It couldn't be too soon to start.

It usually takes—what? A year before a man thinks of marrying again? She braced her shoulders. Well, she was sure Harry would see the sense in marrying a nurse—he wasn't a fool. And she would stay by him always. She would never, never leave him; she would be an asset to him. After all . . . he couldn't see her.

She arrived back at the hospital buoyant, more optimistic

than she had been since she had left Harry's house. She nodded to herself approvingly as she went through the hall and the receptionist looked at her curiously. Carmichael coloured.

"I was just thinking, nearly aloud," she said, almost apologetically.

The receptionist, not used to such amiability from Carmichael replied. "Yes, Miss Carmichael, I thought you were. You looked very pleased."

Carmichael nodded and went on to the office to spend the rest of the day doing her paper work and doing her ward and departmental rounds with a very unusual geniality that surprised everybody. They were used to a much more dogmatic and difficult Carmichael. But today she seemed all sweetness and light. How could they know she was living for five o'clock, living for the time when she could go back to her flat and get ready—put on a dress more suitable and call at the Maitlands' house. That was all she was living for all day, and every time she thought of it her heart lifted.

CHAPTER 25

At six-thirty Carmichael arrived. She rang the bell and waited, thinking they may be out, perhaps at Margaret Tarrant's house. Oh God, she hadn't thought of that. Then she was reassured as she heard footsteps inside the house, and the door opened. It was an unknown man. He looked at her enquiringly.

"I'm Agnes Carmichael. I was here when Mrs. Maitland fell and I've come to see . . ."

He stood back politely and nodded. "I am just going. I called in to see how Harry is. I'm James Hill."

Carmichael nodded self consciously. "Yes, Mr. Hill," she said.

She longed for the ability to say something lighter, like "Oh, are you from the University?" Anything; but would it be right? She followed the man across the hall, and as she did so, the grandfather clock chimed half past six. She had come, surely, at the right time. Harry half rose as she entered the room, but it was Margaret who spoke.

"Ah Agnes, you've come back. How kind—to see how we're faring? Not a very good day, I'm afraid."

Before Carmichael could reply, the man called Hill broke in. "Well, I must go, old man. You're in good hands with Margaret. Good-bye and again I'm so sorry. If there's anything Candy or I can do, please let us know."

Harry nodded. He looked tired. Carmichael noted this with some satisfaction; perhaps he had missed her.

"I'll let myself out. 'Bye. Good-bye, Miss . . ." He had obviously forgotten Carmichael's name. Well, he would, she thought bitterly. Everyone does. But Harry's not going to—I'll see to that.

She took Harry's hand. "I felt I must come and see how you were."

Harry responded to her clasp. "It's so kind of you, Agnes," he said and proceeded to tell her a little about the day.

She sat down beside him and Margaret went and poured a glass of sherry without asking Carmichael and put it down in front of her. Carmichael looked up, thanked her, and went on listening to Harry.

"What an awful day you've had. And the funeral?"

"The funeral is on Thursday. Cremation—that's what she wanted. She always said that."

Harry's voice faltered slightly and he turned away from Carmichael. Immediately Margaret Tarrant was there, her hand on his shoulder. He bent his head sideways and his cheek caressed Margaret's hand.

It was almost too much for Carmichael. She felt at that moment that she could have stabbed Margaret Tarrant through the heart if she'd had a knife in her hand. She was frightened for a moment at the strength of her own feeling.

"Oh, by the way, you left your dress in the wardrobe. Did you know?" Margaret Tarrant's voice was quiet and kind.

Carmichael nodded. "Yes, indeed. I realized it when I went back to my flat and unpacked. I'll fetch it, if I may."

"No, no. I'll go up and get it for you." Margaret Tarrant left the room immediately and Carmichael was left for a precious moment with Harry alone.

She felt sure that now he would ask her to stay for dinner, but all he said was "Has Margaret given you a drink?"

"Yes, thank you," Carmichael replied and picked up the untouched sherry and sipped it. Now, surely he will say . . . now, surely. After all, she hadn't got anything in her flat for the evening meal. Not that he would know that, of course.

"Margaret has been an absolute staff and prop. She's a wonderful person. I don't know but she seems to know exactly what one wants and anticipates it."

"I'm glad," Carmichael's voice was cold, but Harry did not appear to notice.

"Here we are." Margaret walked in the room carrying a carrier from a famous shop. "I've packed it carefully with tissue paper. It's such a pretty dress."

Carmichael took the bag and put it down beside her. Now they'd ask her, now. She tried to will them to. She looked at the clock. It was almost seven. What time did they eat?

"Are you eating yet? Have you managed to . . . ?"

"A little. Margaret's seen to that."

"Oh, I've been very bossy with him, poor love. I'm making him do as he's told. He must, I'm afraid."

"What about the test and this evening's insulin?" Carmichael asked and she heard the voice of the nurse speaking and wished she could cut it out.

"Oh, that's all right. Maurice has been and done what is necessary. I can give the insulin. I've done it before when Emily has been away. I don't like doing it, but I told Maurice I would and I'm getting used to it. Don't worry." Margaret Tarrant's voice, light and charming as usual, was obviously quite unaware of how Carmichael was longing to be asked to stay.

"Another sherry?" She had not noticed the fact that Carmichael's glass was hardly touched.

At last Carmichael realized she was not going to be asked to dinner. It was no use. These people were not like her. They were refined.

She was silent, thinking to herself that Margaret Tarrant would have laid the table in the dining room, or Mrs. Greenwood would have done so for her, with the right plates, the right cutlery, the right glasses for the right wine. It was impossible. Carmichael would never learn. Her rival sat opposite her, with her beautiful white hair, elegant clothes, and what Carmichael felt was a kind of unconscious arrogance—knowing what to do and when to do it. Carmichael got up abruptly.

"I must be going then." She felt she sounded like Mrs. Greenwood.

"Don't forget your bag," Margaret Tarrant said and Harry rose too, and they both accompanied her to the front door.

"It was sweet of you to come," said Margaret Tarrant and Harry spoke too.

"Yes, indeed. It's nice when people show concern. I hope you'll come again."

"I will, I will," Carmichael said and she walked out of the

front door and along to her Mini, feeling that they would not shut the door until they had seen her get into her car.

She was right. As she slammed the car door she heard the front door close and she realized suddenly that she had not offered again to give Harry his insulin. Well, Margaret Tarrant said she could give it. As she started up the engine she hoped that Margaret would hurt Harry, even though Carmichael couldn't bear the thought of him being hurt. She hoped she wouldn't give it properly, that the insulin would squirt out of the syringe and not go into his arm, that she wouldn't put the needle on the syringe firmly. All this might be bad for Harry, but it would be good for Agnes. It would make him realize . . .

Even if she, Carmichael, didn't know all she should about wine, etiquette, introducing people, painting, music, she did at least know how to look after and treat a diabetic. If Margaret Tarrant did something terribly wrong—didn't get the doctor in time and Harry died—unstable as his diabetes was at the moment, there was a risk—if she did that, Carmichael felt she would surely kill her.

CHAPTER 26

Next morning Carmichael's undulating confidence returned again. She felt that she had been underestimating herself. Her walk about the hospital, became more decided; her amiability receded. The staff resignedly thought that she was going back to her old ways. The story of her horrifying weekend was now hospital property—old gossip.

In the Children's Ward, she was condescending to Sister Jones. She'd seen little of her in the last week. Jones looked at her curiously and, contrary to her usual practice, made a personal remark.

"You look different, Miss Carmichael," she said.

"Do I?" Carmichael sounded interested. "In what way?"

"I don't know, sort of . . . as if something nice had happened, as if you'd been left a fortune—something like that." Carmichael smiled.

"Perhaps I have," she said primly and then, in a sudden burst of confiding, "I'll tell you about it at lunchtime in the rest room, if we can find a corner to ourselves."

Jones nodded, her eyes lighting up with interest. Since the death of her mother, she had not made the social contacts she had hoped. Perhaps it was years of having been tied down, imprisoned.

Carmichael left the ward. Jones' remark had given her confidence, a further lift. Why did she disparage herself? After all, look what she'd done for Jones. Should she give her a hint? She smiled again, walking along the corridor, her step firm.

It was true; she did continually disparage herself. It was nothing, nothing, the difference between her and this Margaret Tarrant. After all, Margaret Tarrant wouldn't know what to do if Harry went into a coma. She'd just flap around, ring the doctor.

She, Carmichael, could bring him back to life, if necessary; she could save him.

Once he was married to her, he need never worry again. She wondered if they would sleep together? Emily's room had twin beds—that would be perfect, she thought. Now Emily was gone, he would go up to his own bedroom. As she walked along the hospital corridor she thought of going to bed beside him, the bedside lamp lighted between them. And at the thought of the lamp . . . who else could think of something like that, something to get rid of a person without a trace? She laughed softly.

Two nurses scurrying past her looked at her apprehensively and one remarked, "She's mad, old Carmichael, she's barmy."

The remark did not offend Carmichael in the least. In fact, she was somewhat amused. She was too complacent at the moment to be offended by anything.

At lunch she sat at a table with Jones and two other Sisters. After they'd finished, they all four left the dining room. Luckily the other two made for the changing room and Jones and Carmichael walked upstairs to the Sisters' rest room. Carmichael waited until the orderly had brought in their coffee and plonked it down on their table.

"Well?" said Jones. "What's all this about? Have you got a secret you haven't told me? Is it to do with Professor Maitland?"

"How did you know?" Carmichael was almost skittish and Jones, seeing that the point needed pressing, went on.

"It is. You're not—you're not—having an affair with him, are you? I mean, before his wife . . . were you?"

Carmichael did not answer for a moment or two. She sat sipping her coffee, her eyes cast down, thinking: Shall I . . . say I was having an affair with him before Emily died? Would it be a good idea? Then, if he did ask me to marry him rather sooner than a year, it would make it better. But then, would I like anyone to think that Harry would have an affair with anyone? No, his name was sacrosanct. She looked up and the concentration and the coffee had brought a blush to her pasty cheeks.

Jones noticed it. "Oh, it is to do with him, isn't it—you've gone quite pink." She giggled.

Carmichael looked round as two more Sisters came in, but

they went and sat over in the far corner, well away from them. The room was large and Carmichael thought it was quite safe to carry on the conversation without them hearing.

"Well, in a way. There's no doubt about it—he does . . . he is fond of me. I've noticed it, you know. He takes my hand whenever he can, sits close to me, that kind of thing. I don't mean that he . . . I think it's just a natural fondness."

"Did he get on well with his wife?"

Carmichael shook her head. "No, she was a selfish woman, continually thinking about her painting—she was no good at painting, you know."

Carmichael wondered if she should mention the young men and decided against it. No, it might get back to Harry that she had been gossiping; or even to Margaret Tarrant, who she felt sure would never do such a thing. No, this was part of learning how "they" behaved. She decided to say nothing about Jeremy and the others. Jones nodded, sagely, as if she knew all about this kind of affair, which made Carmichael smile. However, the next remark Jones made shattered Carmichael.

"About Mother." Jones paused. She put down her coffee cup and started again obviously with an effort, but still with determination. "About Mother. I always feel . . . I'm never sure . . . I don't quite know what to say, Agnes, but I've always felt it was strange how she died that night you were there."

Carmichael became quite still. Was Jones going to accuse her of killing her mother?

"I mean, it was funny that she died when you were there— like Professor Maitland's wife."

Carmichael stiffened. She spoke, perhaps too hastily.

"Well, Emily's death was nothing to do with me. I was giving Harry his injection," she said.

"Oh, I didn't mean that. I mean it was awful for you, being there. But then, of course, you didn't know Mother was going to die."

Carmichael looked up and met Jones' eyes and suddenly suspected that she knew that she, Carmichael, had given her mother an overdose, or at least knew that she was capable of it.

After all, she had suggested . . . She felt uncertain what to say to Jones next and decided to play it very lightly.

"Yes, people had better be careful around me, hadn't they? Two have died while I've been in their houses—well, not your mother, but after I'd been in her house."

The direct approach stilled Jones' tongue for a moment and she sat silent, her own colour mounting as Carmichael's had done, but for a different reason.

"Oh, I didn't mean anything. I was just thinking . . . that it was odd, you know," said Jones, lamely.

"Well, you should be very thankful if I have this effect on people. It's a load lifted from you—at least you can lead your own life now."

"I know, but I miss her and it's not easy to . . . Shall we go out and have a meal sometime in town . . . ?"

Carmichael shook her head. "I think I shall be rather busy, but perhaps I'll try and squeeze it in one evening." Her voice was patronizing. "I must get back now. They're short in Out Patients and I shall have to keep an eye on them this afternoon. They've got four Clinics and that Varicose Vein Clinic takes at least three nurses, with the new treatment they're giving."

Jones nodded absently. "Yes, I must get back too."

She rose with difficulty from her chair. She was fatter than ever, Carmichael thought, since her mother died, and she looked complacently down at her own slim body. I've got a good figure, she thought and turned on her heel and walked out of the door, conscious of Jones' eyes following her.

CHAPTER 27

Carmichael arrived in Out Patients about an hour later. The four Clinics had started. There were very few vacant seats in the waiting room. Carmichael went round to check who had arrived. She always drew the nurses aside to ask what time a Consultant had come—late or punctually—and usually the nurse lied to her, said the Consultant had arrived on time. This Carmichael regarded as misplaced loyalty and felt nothing but contempt for the nurse who tried to protect the doctor for whom she was working.

The only one who had not arrived was the Ear, Nose, and Throat Surgeon—he was invariably late. Carmichael tut-tutted and told the nurse that if he didn't come within half an hour to ring her. The nurse nodded and sat down in the examination room and started swinging round and round in the chair meant for the patient directly Carmichael had left the room. Carmichael knew this because she heard the squeak of the chair and she turned back and went into the Clinic room. The nurse sprang up as Carmichael walked in.

"I would oil that, nurse. Don't waste your time. Surely there is a can of oil somewhere, or you could put a little liquid paraffin round it. It must be very annoying for the Consultant and the patient as well."

"I will, Miss Carmichael, I will. I'll get some liquid paraffin and put round the . . ." She looked uncertainly at the base of the chair.

"Well, don't drop any on the floor and cause the patient to slip."

Carmichael swept out and went back into the Sister's office, where the list of Clinics lay on the table. She looked down at them. Each Clinic was pretty full—they'd be hard put to it to get through by half past five and that would mean trouble. The Path. Lab. the Records office—they all liked to get off at five, not to speak of X-ray. That would mean some of the patients who were seen late would not get any of the tests done that were needed and would have to come back.

Carmichael looked up, and through the glass window of Sister's office, to her surprise she saw, sitting near the Canteen, Mrs. Greenwood stirring a cup of tea, obviously waiting to go into one of the Clinics. At that moment Mrs. Greenwood looked up and their eyes met. Carmichael felt she must go over and speak to her. She felt sure that this was how Margaret Tarrant would behave; but then, Margaret Tarrant wouldn't be a Nursing Officer, wouldn't know how to be. She crossed the waiting room, stood in front of Mrs. Greenwood, who looked at her with decidedly more respect than she had in the kitchen of the Maitlands' house.

"Oh, it's Nurse Carmichael. Don't you look different in that dress and—"

"It's Miss Carmichael. I'm a Nursing Officer, not a nurse," said Carmichael briskly.

She felt so different, so much raised up above Mrs. Greenwood's level, it gave her pleasure and she decided that she would talk to Mrs. Greenwood. Since she was a Nursing Officer, that was perfectly correct. She would be careful though, what she said. She sat down on the vacant chair beside Mrs. Greenwood.

"What Clinic are you waiting for?"

"Oh, Mr. Exstead. I'm having me veins done. Well, they're going to inject them. I'm not looking forward to it. I've had them done before and it hurt—didn't do much good either—they've come back. But I thought I'd have another go. I don't want the operation—I'm frightened of anaesthetics." Mrs. Greenwood was voluble, but respectful.

Carmichael nodded understandingly. "Well, there's nothing to be afraid of if you do have the operation, but the injections should work. I can't think why they didn't." Carmichael felt a slur on her profession was implied.

Mrs. Greenwood nodded. "Perhaps they will this time—I hope so, anyway."

"How is Professor Maitland? Did you see him this morning?"

"Yes. He's not too bad. Better, now Mrs. Tarrant's moved in. I'm only there till twelve. It's nice having her there—she's a real lady, Mrs. Tarrant. I've always liked her—so does the Professor." She glanced sideways at Carmichael with a peculiar smile.

Whether people in the social strata to which Carmichael was aiming gossiped was dismissed from Carmichael's mind. She felt she must know more about the household—what it was like before Emily's death.

She said, almost tentatively, "Well, the Professor can't miss his wife all that much, if she was, as you said, always out and about and having affairs."

"So she was. Having affairs," said Mrs. Greenwood, obviously eager to talk. "I mean, those young men—you can't keep them, you see, not when you're fifty; and she was that, if she was a day. They used to come to her, say they wanted to paint and how good they were and nobody would give them a chance. Then she'd talk about her protégé and have a cocktail party for them, invite other painters to meet them. I used to do some of the parties. I knew them. Simpering young things. One or two of them were good-looking. Awful for Professor Maitland, the way she used to fuss over them and kiss them—in front of him. Not that he took much notice. Well, he found his consolation somewhere else."

Carmichael turned sharply and gazed directly at Mrs. Greenwood. "Found his consolation? What do you mean?"

Mrs. Greenwood was so enjoying the conversation that she had let her tea get cold, forgetting even about her coming injection. She gazed at Carmichael knowingly.

"We-e-ll, Margaret Tarrant was, wasn't she? Had been ever since her husband died. I was glad. I used to say to myself, Well, you won't care about Emily and her little boys. That's all they were really."

What did she mean, consolation? Could it be that Harry and Margaret Tarrant . . . was he in love with her?

"He's very fond of Mrs. Tarrant then?" Carmichael ventured.

"Fond! More than that. Often when Emily was away with her paramours," said Mrs. Greenwood, "Margaret Tarrant used to stay the weekend. Oh, I think Emily knew that, but didn't give a damn. That move downstairs—I knew all about that. Gave me two rooms to do instead of one. It was all because at one week-end Emily got a bit pie-eyed at one of her parties and the Professor found her in bed with—I don't remember his name—Cecil, I think. I thought he was a poof, but he wasn't."

Carmichael prayed that no one would call from Mr. Exstead's Clinic and ask Mrs. Greenwood to go in.

"That was the beginning of it, see?"

Carmichael nodded. She felt dulled by this torrent of conversation that was telling her things that she didn't want to know.

"I can't believe that Professor Maitland—that he or Mrs. Tarrant would . . . She seems a very nice lady." Carmichael realized that she was speaking like Mrs. Greenwood—"that nice lady"—exactly the kind of term Mrs. Greenwood would use.

"Oh, she is. She's lovely and I believe she's very much in love with Professor Maitland and as soon as it's decent they'll marry. Her husband was at the University. They like the same things."

Carmichael felt sick—she had to believe it. There was a ring of truth in Mrs. Greenwood's voice and what sounded like a real affection for Harry and no dislike for the woman who for some time might have been his mistress, in the place of a wife who had cuckolded him and meant nothing to him.

"He told me Emily was beautiful—I mean when they . . . I reckon she was. She was good-looking right up to . . . Funny that, the way she fell down the stairs. After all, it's made it all come right, like a love story, hasn't it?" said Mrs. Greenwood with relish.

At that moment a nurse came to the Clinic door and called, "Mrs. Greenwood, please."

Mrs. Greenwood got up, hastily bending down by the side of her chair and picking up her handbag and head scarf. "Oh, Lord, hope it's not going to hurt like it did last time," she said.

Carmichael made reassuring noises and Mrs. Greenwood nodded. "It's helped pass the time, anyway, talking to you." It was evident that Mrs. Greenwood was rather pleased that the other patients round had seen her talking to someone who was obviously important in the hospital.

"Will you come round again, Miss Carmichael?" she asked. Carmichael nodded.

"Yes, I will," she said and saw Mrs. Greenwood disappear into the Clinic room.

"I've been here an hour. Will they keep me waiting much longer, miss?" A voice said plaintively and Carmichael turned aside to a patient who was sitting on the edge of her chair, a plastic handbag clutched on her knee.

Carmichael saw the marks of sweat on the handbag from the woman's fingers. "What Clinic are you for and what time is your appointment?"

"It was for half past two and it's half past three."

Carmichael nodded and was about to go to the office where the Out Patient Sister stood looking at the list, but suddenly she couldn't. She could not go back to mundane things—she had got to go somewhere quiet so that she could digest what she had heard. She had to get somewhere away from people; she couldn't face her own office.

She went into the Sisters' changing room and stood in front of the glass looking at her full length. The nurses were supposed to check their uniform in this mirror—the Sisters too—before they left the room. Carmichael thought she looked nice in her dark blue dress; but what did all that matter if Harry and Margaret Tarrant were lovers? She heard the handle of the changing room turn and she went into the lavatory and sat down on the seat, locking the door.

She tried to picture them together. She thought again of Emily's bedroom, of the two beds, the lamp. Am I wrong? Is Mrs. Greenwood wrong? Is all this nonsense? Is this how these people live, maintaining a dignified silence about each others vagaries? "We each go our own way, we lead our own lives"— how many times had she seen that in gossip columns. Well, this was the kind of thing gossip columns were about. It was not her life—brought up in an orphanage, not any background, no parents—how could she ever know? Then school, back to the orphanage, then into hospital as a cadet, then later taking up her training, leaving the orphanage. Her life flashed in front of her, there in the lavatory, rather like before death, she thought. But whose? She couldn't let this happen, not Margaret Tarrant and Harry. No, she couldn't.

Carmichael got up, unlocked the door. Whoever had come into the changing room had left. The place was empty. She walked out like an automaton, back to her office. She knew exactly what she had to do. She must plan carefully, much more carefully than she had ever planned before.

"What's Out Patients like—a rugger scrum as usual?" Johnson said. "Ear, Nose, and Throat Clinic on Wednesday afternoon, isn't it? That never starts on time. There's always an excuse, isn't there? Epistaxis—every E.N.T. man in the world uses that excuse. I suppose it's better than any other. After all, no one can say he's a liar, can they? If he says he's got a bleeder—'bleeder' being the operative word—he could come in covered in blood if he wanted to—make it more authentic." Johnson laughed.

Carmichael looked at her dully. What was she saying—nose bleeding? "Yes, that's right," she said and Johnson looked at her with curiosity.

Carmichael could tell she was thinking, Queer one she is; what's the matter with her? But she didn't mind; she didn't mind any more what people thought of her.

"I may not be in tomorrow," she said. Johnson looked up in surprise.

"Oh, have you asked for the day off?"

"No, I haven't asked, but I just don't think I'll be in. If anyone asks, say I'm not well."

"Aren't you?"

But Carmichael only shook her head. "I didn't say that. Just say it for me, if you don't mind."

"Well, you'd better ring me up in the morning or something and say you're not well. Then I can say it with some truth. Something special?"

Carmichael nodded. "Yes, something special," she said and her tone made Johnson ask no more questions.

Carmichael took a long drive after duty. She went along the country roads over the Downs and when she got to the top of the hill, she drove the Mini into a lay-by and put down the window. The wind blew into the car bringing a perfume with it of earth and grass. The wind was cold, but Carmichael hardly noticed it. She sat there a long time, gazing out across the valley to the river. It glittered in the moonlight and looked like glass, grey glass. Further along, as her eyes moved, she saw a similar glitter from a row of greenhouses. They, too, looked like water. It was like a huge garden.

I loved all this before, before I met Harry, Carmichael thought. She felt he had done her an irreparable injury. There had been so much to be proud of. Her job, her flat, her car—and Tibbles. Everything had been such a step up, such a huge step up. She had got what she wanted, even the companionship of her little cat. If she'd never met Harry, she would have perhaps taken a foreign holiday, had a nice time, made more friends. Harry had stopped all that. I hate them, she thought, coupling the two together, Margaret and Harry. She hated them and everything they stood for—culture, knowledge of how to behave. She had come far, a long way from the orphanage. She'd done well, very well. But one look from those blind eyes, one touch of that hand, and it had been swept away. She must put it right. She must make both of them pay for what they had done to her.

As she sat there, she remembered Jones' look of knowledge, as if she had realized that the overdose had been given by Carmichael to her mother. Well, it had. She was powerful in her own way, she had more power than any of them. But it was no good now, no good at least to make a life with Harry. The power she had could be used, but only to destroy.

Carmichael took her eyes away from the view, not appreciating it any more. She remembered that she had brought a picnic up here in the summer and so loved it. Yes, they had done this to her, they had done it all. She turned the key in the ignition and the engine started sweetly. She had loved her little car, but not any more. She turned the car round, left the lay-by, drove down hill, back to town. She had at least a three-quarters-of-an-hour drive, but she didn't enjoy it as she usually did—even that enjoyment had been taken away from her. She went faster. She felt the tears pouring down her cheeks. She must get home—there was the cat to feed.

CHAPTER 28

The next day Carmichael did not go in for duty—this was the first time in the whole of her nursing career she had stayed away without reason. She did not ring Johnson. Let her handle it as she would and let the seniors handle it how they would too. Carmichael no longer cared.

She got up late, fed Tibbles, and took her along to Mrs. Jenks.

"Of course. Going out again? Got some time off?" said Mrs. Jenks, taking Tibbles from Carmichael's arms. The cat purred loudly and rubbed the top of her head against Mrs. Jenks' chin. After all, thought Carmichael, dumbly, she sees more of her than she does me.

"Yes, I'm going into the country for the day," she said.

After a sleepless night, her eyes felt hot and burning. She put out a hand and stroked the cat, gently, in Mrs. Jenks' arms. She went back into her flat and remembered she hadn't given Mrs. Jenks any food for Tibbles, but then, she could fetch it if she wanted it; there was plenty here and she'd got the key.

Carmichael made herself a cup of tea and sat gazing out of the window, letting the tea cool beside her. Then, she got up, looked round the flat, went into the kitchen to see that she had not left the stove on. As she was about to make her way out, she suddenly had an idea and came back and picked up the telephone directory. She flicked through the book, looking for the name—M. Tarrant—found it and noted the address. She wanted communication, contact, with the two people who meant the most in her life and who had altered it so completely—first with the woman who could deny her everything, then with the man.

She drove the Mini out of the garage, paused a moment wondering where to go first, and decided she would look at Margaret Tarrant's house. She arrived at the row of houses set back from

the road, drove the car slowly along until she found the name of
the house, st. malo. There it was in the winter sunlight, similar
to the Maitlands' house. She parked the car and looked down the
drive that sloped slightly from the road in a wide sweep to the
house itself. She sat there for a long time, wondering, Was Margaret Tarrant there? Should she go and knock on the door and
find out? She was suddenly startled by a man walking across the
drive with a wheelbarrow and spade, the handle sticking out at
the side. He didn't glance towards the car. The gardener. The
fact that there was someone there was reassuring. Should she
. . . ? She got out of the car, crossed the road, and walked down
the sloping drive, her feet making a crunching noise. She
stopped at the door and rang the bell. For some time no one
answered, then the door opened.

"Yes?" The woman had an overall on and was wearing rubber
gloves. She looked neither pleased nor displeased; just blank.
The Help—the Mrs. Greenwood of St. Malo, thought Carmichael.

"Is Mrs. Tarrant in?"

"No, she's not in. She's away." Carmichael knew where she
was, but she wanted to find out more.

"Oh, I wanted to see her. Will she be away long?"

"I don't know. She didn't say when she'd be back."

"Oh, I see. What a nuisance. Do you know where I can get
hold of her? Her telephone number or where she's staying or
anything?" The woman suddenly looked guarded and answered
almost abruptly.

"No, no, I don't know where Mrs. Tarrant is. Staying with a
friend, I think." Carmichael stared past the woman into the
shady hall. It gleamed, the floor shining and reflecting the furniture. A costly house with costly furnishings.

"Well, never mind. I'll call back later. In a day or two, would
you think?" The woman shook her head.

This time she was more brusque. "I've no idea, I really
haven't. I just come to clean and I'm afraid I can't help you."

She closed the door and Carmichael walked up the drive,
crossed the path, and got into her car. She sat quite a time, not
caring if the woman looked out of the window and saw her still

sitting there. What did it matter? she thought, she was no one. "I don't know when she'll be back" . . . Probably never. Margaret would sell that house for a lot of money and move in with Harry for ever—that's what she'd do.

Carmichael started the car and drove back into the town. It was nearly lunchtime. She parked the car and went into a café and ordered lunch. Fish. When she got it and had taken the first mouthful she found she could not swallow it. She didn't want to let anyone see her, having ordered the meal, not eating it, so she toyed with the food for a long time.

At last the waitress came up and said, "Is something wrong?"

Carmichael looked up, her eyes hardly focussing. "Oh, no, it's just that I'm not as hungry as I thought."

The waitress looked at her curiously. "Oh, I'm sorry. I thought perhaps there was something wrong with the fish," she said.

Carmichael shook her head.

"Would you have some coffee then?"

Carmichael nodded and after a few minutes the girl put a cup of coffee down in front of her with the bill and took away the plate of almost untouched fish. Carmichael did not open the folded bill that the girl placed beside her on a plate.

"Are you all right, miss? I mean, do you feel all right?"

Carmichael looked up sharply. "Why, what do you mean? Why do you ask that?"

"Well, you're a bit pale and you didn't eat your lunch and I thought perhaps you weren't well."

"I'm quite all right." Carmichael's voice was sharp, but then she looked at the waitress' concerned face and thought well, at least she cared, so she amended her words a little.

"Thank you," she said. She finished her coffee, went to the cash desk, paid her bill, aware that the waitress' curious eyes were still on her, and then she left.

CHAPTER 29

For some time no one answered the doorbell. Carmichael looked at her watch. Six-thirty—about the right time to come. This afternoon had dragged interminably, but now it was over. Suddenly the door opened. It was not Margaret Tarrant as she had expected; it was Harry.

"It's Agnes. I've just come to see how you are. I thought I must know."

"Do come in. How nice of you to come. We've had rather a nasty experience here," he said, walking towards the sitting room, Carmichael following him.

"What's happened? Have you . . . Is your . . . ?"

"No, not me. It's Margaret. I did something so stupid, I can't forgive myself."

"Yes, you can darling. It was no one's fault. Anyone could have done it." It was Margaret Tarrant's voice. She was sitting on the settee, her face paler than usual, her right hand resting on her lap. The forefinger and middle finger of the hand were bandaged.

She looked up, smiling. "We've just got back from your Casualty department. We wondered if we'd see you."

Carmichael shook her head. "I haven't been in today," she said.

"So silly. I shut my hand in the car door—painful—I had to have a couple of stitches and I'm a dreadful coward. It's put me out of action a little—"

Harry would not let her go on. "Why not tell Agnes the truth, darling? It wasn't you who shut your hand in the door, it was I. Oh, God, sometimes my sightlessness . . . Margaret was kindly shepherding me into her car. I didn't realize her hand was still on the door jamb and I pulled the door shut."

Margaret Tarrant looked quizzically at Carmichael. "It hurt a bit, but it doesn't now. They gave me two injections."

Carmichael nodded. "Antitetanus and an antibiotic, I expect," she said, primly.

"It would have been nice to see you there. We hoped we would. But I expect your duties are administrative—you would hardly be in Casualty."

"I'm in charge of that department, but I've been off today. How have you been, Harry? I mean, the diabetes? Have you suffered at all with all these crises? One sometimes finds that it unstabilizes one more . . ." Carmichael suddenly felt incoherent.

It was Margaret Tarrant who answered. "Yes, I'm afraid it's made things a bit worse. There's a problem I wonder if you would help us with." She smiled at Carmichael her charming smile. "Doctor came and Harry had to have some tests—blood tests. They've changed his insulin—he's having a little more, morning and evening now. This evening I won't be able to give it with my hand like this. I was going to ring up the District Nurse—I didn't want to worry Maurice again; he's terribly busy. Do you think—?"

Carmichael broke in quickly. "I'll give it, of course. What time?"

"Oh, not yet. About seven o'clock. Mrs. Greenwood has kindly said she'd come back." Almost as she said it there was the sound of a key in the front door. "There she is. She's going to do the evening meal. I don't think I could peel potatoes with this."

She comically held up her two bandaged fingers. "Dollies. That's what my children used to call them when they were little." Carmichael nodded and Mrs. Greenwood appeared at the sitting room door.

"How are you then? Oh, I am sorry—look at that!" She cast a sympathetic look at Margaret's hand.

"I'm so glad we were able to get hold of you, Mrs. Greenwood. Thank goodness you're on the phone. We wouldn't have been able to eat tonight unless we'd gone out and I don't honestly feel very much like that."

Mrs. Greenwood nodded. "Of course not. I'll make something. It had better be something you won't have to cut up. I'll see what there is in the freezer."

"Perhaps there's some minced beef or something, and we could have that."

"I know—I'll make a nice cottage pie. That'll do. It'll be easy to eat and I can put very little potato on top so that the Professor can have it. I'll see to everything. Don't you worry." She bustled off and Carmichael heard her go upstairs and wondered vaguely why.

Quite suddenly, it came to Carmichael—what she had to do and the wonderful opportunity she had been given to do it. She felt the room receding from her, a whistling in her ears. She felt she was going to faint.

"Are you all right, Agnes? You've gone awfully pale."

Carmichael shook her head vigorously. "No, I'm all right, perfectly all right, thank you. If I might . . ." She looked toward the hall and Margaret nodded.

"Well, of course. You're sure you're . . ." she said.

Carmichael nodded again, walked to the door, crossed the hall, and into the downstairs cloakroom. She went in and closed the door. She had got to recover. She looked in the mirror. Her lips were as white as her cheeks. She rubbed her face vigorously with her hands, sat down on the lavatory seat, and put her head between her knees. After a little while, she was able to go back into the sitting room. Mrs. Greenwood came downstairs as she walked across the hall and went into the kitchen.

"All right?" Margaret Tarrant looked at her anxiously.

"Perfectly all right, thank you, perfectly."

"You'll stay to dinner of course," Margaret Tarrant said, but Carmichael shook her head hastily.

"No, if you don't mind, I won't. I've got things to do. I will have a drink, though. Then after I've given Harry his insulin, I'll go." Her voice had a finality in it that Margaret Tarrant recognized.

"What would you like?" Margaret Tarrant asked.

Carmichael looked up and said firmly, "I'd like a brandy."

Harry's face registered slight surprise and Margaret Tarrant spoke quickly. "I don't think Agnes felt awfully well just now. A brandy will be just the thing."

Carmichael nodded. She certainly felt she must have something to make her feel less strange. The drink was put down in front of her. Margaret got a drink for Harry and one for herself.

Carmichael drank the brandy quickly. It did make her feel better. She got to her feet almost at once.

"Well, I'll give the insulin," she said.

Harry too, stood up. "Thank you, I'm so grateful."

Carmichael preceded him out of the sitting room and made her way across to his room, but he stopped her.

"No, it's upstairs now, upstairs in the bathroom."

Was there a slight self-consciousness in his voice? Carmichael couldn't be sure. "Are you sure you can manage the stairs?"

There was a hint of sarcasm in Carmichael's voice, but he seemed not to notice it and followed her up the stairs easily. He motioned towards the bathroom and the sight of the twin beds made Carmichael feel faint and sick. The coverlets had been turned back, presumably by Mrs. Greenwood.

Carmichael went through into the bathroom and opened the cabinet, the same cabinet as she had opened to find the codeine for Emily. There was the insulin, the syringe, the spirit bottle, the swabs, everything—put there, of course, by Margaret. Carmichael took the syringe from the cabinet, swabbed the top of the insulin bottle with spirit, and drove home the needle through the cap of the bottle.

"How many units?" she asked and Harry told her.

Carmichael drew six times the amount out of the bottle. Indeed, she almost emptied it. She approached Harry who was standing, his jacket off, shirt sleeve rolled up. She plunged the needle straight into his arm. He winced.

"That hurt more than usual, Agnes. It smarted a bit," he said and Carmichael murmured, "Sorry."

She looked at his face. That should be enough, she thought. Insulin coma—death—and the doctor busy on a round. Oh, there'd be another doctor, but he wouldn't live next door but one. Harry rolled down his sleeve, put on his coat, and followed her down the stairs.

"All done," he said, coming into the sitting room. He bent down suddenly, feeling for Margaret Tarrant's hand, and kissed her, she offering her lips. It was done unselfconsciously and without guilt. Well, enjoy each other while you can, Carmichael thought. She felt triumphant now, confident. The faintness had completely disappeared.

She said a hasty good-bye and Margaret Tarrant saw her to the front door. As she did so, Carmichael could hear Mrs. Greenwood clattering about in the kitchen. She turned once more. She could see Harry through the sitting-room door. She noticed he was rubbing his arm, as if the injection still hurt him. Well, it might.

"Good-bye, Harry," she said and went back, took his hand, and pressed it for the last time. But she felt no feeling of sorrow, nothing at all.

In her Mini she drove and drove, into the darkness, her headlights lighting up the road in front of her. Indeed, the lights seemed to be leading her, rather than she driving the car. From the town to the country, towards the river. At last she arrived. She turned off the road, down to the river's edge, the car skidding a little on the wet grass, her headlights, for the moment, lighting up the river. She knew it was deep here. They'd had a drowning in, from almost this very spot, into Casualty months ago. She peered up and down the river. To her right she could see the silhouette of the willows, bare against the sky. She leaned over and opened the other window. The cold wind rushed into the car. She took off the brake, put out her car lights, and the car eased gently forward, down into the river.

At first, Carmichael felt a sensation of floating, then the little car began to settle. The green water of the river flowed in through both windows. As the car sank deeper, Carmichael thought, This is how . . . Then she didn't think any more . . . The river closed over the top of the Mini, its green waters swirling a little in the darkness.

February 2nd. Item from the local paper.

Due to the prompt action of the St. John Ambulance Brigade, who, fortunately, were in the vicinity returning from an emergency call, a local Nurse had a miraculous escape from drowning.

She was trapped in her submerged car which had apparently gone out of control and plunged into the river.

Charles Morgan, Ambulance Driver, said, "It was touch and go. The lady was already unconscious when I managed to get her out. Fortunately I am a fairly strong swimmer."

Miss Agnes Carmichael was taken to the local hospital.

On May 25th the marriage took place between Mrs. Margaret Tarrant and Professor Harry Maitland at Dwyford Registry Office. Only a few friends were present and a small dinner party was held at the University afterwards. The couple left for a honeymoon in the Seychelles.

ABOUT THE AUTHOR

ANTHEA COHEN trained as a nurse at Leicester Royal Infirmary. For the past twenty-five years she has worked, on and off, in hospitals and as a private nurse. She has written on medicine and hospital life, been a columnist for *Nursing Mirror*, and has contributed regularly to *World Medicine*. She has published innumerable short stories and is a popular author of books for the teenage market in the United States. *Angel of Death* is her third novel for the Crime Club.